Fierce

Darkest Night Series, Volume 5

Lexy Timms

Published by Dark Shadow Publishing, 2020.

This is a work of fiction. Similarities to real people, places, or events are entirely coincidental.

FIERCE

First edition. September 15, 2020.

Copyright © 2020 Lexy Timms.

Written by Lexy Timms.

Also by Lexy Timms

A Bad Boy Bullied Romance
I Hate You
I Hate You A Little Bit
I Hate You A Little Bit More

A Burning Love Series
Spark of Passion
Flame of Desire
Blaze of Ecstasy

A Chance at Forever Series
Forever Perfect
Forever Desired
Forever Together

A Dating App Series
I've Been Matched
You've Been Matched

We've Been Matched

A "Kind of" Billionaire
Taking a Risk
Safety in Numbers
Pretend You're Mine

A Maybe Series
Maybe I Should
Maybe I Shouldn't
Maybe I Did

Assisting the Boss Series
Billion Reasons
Duke of Delegation
Late Night Meetings
Delegating Love
Suitors and Admirers

BBW Romance Series
Capturing Her Beauty
Pursuing Her Dreams
Tracing Her Curves

Beating the Biker Series
Making Her His
Making the Break
Making of Them

Billionaire Banker Series
Banking on Him
Price of Passion
Investing in Love
Knowing Your Worth
Treasured Forever
Banking on Christmas

Billionaire Holiday Romance Series
Driving Home for Christmas
The Valentine Getaway
Cruising Love

Billionaire in Disguise Series
Facade
Illusion
Charade

Billionaire Secrets Series

The Secret
Freedom
Courage
Trust
Impulse
Billionaire Secrets Box Set Books #1-3

Blind Sight Series
See Me
Fix Me
Eyes On Me

Branded Series
Money or Nothing
What People Say
Give and Take

Building Billions
Building Billions - Part 1
Building Billions - Part 2
Building Billions - Part 3

Butler & Heiress Series
To Serve
For Duty
No Chore

Change of Heart Series
The Heart Needs
The Heart Wants
The Heart Knows

Conquering Warrior Series
Ruthless

Counting the Billions
Counting the Days
Counting On You
Counting the Kisses

Darkest Night Series
Savage
Vicious
Brutal
Sinful
Fierce

Diamond in the Rough Anthology
Billionaire Rock
Billionaire Rock - part 2

Dirty Little Taboo Series
Flirting Touch
Denying Pleasure
Forbidding Desire
Craving Passion

Dominating PA Series
Her Personal Assistant - Part 1
Her Personal Assistant Box Set

Fake Billionaire Series
Faking It
Temporary CEO
Caught in the Act
Never Tell A Lie
Fake Christmas
Fake Billionaire Box Set #1-3

Firehouse Romance Series
Caught in Flames
Burning With Desire
Craving the Heat
Firehouse Romance Complete Collection

Forging Billions Series
Dirty Money
Petty Cash
Payment Required

For His Pleasure
Elizabeth
Georgia
Madison

Fortune Riders MC Series
Billionaire Biker
Billionaire Ransom
Billionaire Misery
Fortune Riders Box Set - Books #1-3

Fragile Series
Fragile Touch
Fragile Kiss
Fragile Love

Great Temptation Series
The Devil's Footsteps
Heaven's Command

Mortals Surrender

Hades' Spawn Motorcycle Club
One You Can't Forget
One That Got Away
One That Came Back
One You Never Leave
One Christmas Night
Hades' Spawn MC Complete Series

Hard Rocked Series
Rhyme
Harmony
Lyrics

Heart of Stone Series
The Protector
The Guardian
The Warrior

Heart of the Battle Series
Celtic Viking
Celtic Rune
Celtic Mann
Heart of the Battle Series Box Set

Heistdom Series
Master Thief
Goldmine
Diamond Heist
Smile For Me
Your Move
Green With Envy
Saving Money

Highlander Wolf Series
Pack Run
Pack Land
Pack Rules

How To Love A Spy
The Secret
The Secret Life
The Secret Wife

Just About Series
About Love
About Truth
About Forever
Just About Box Set Books #1-3

Justice Series
Seeking Justice
Finding Justice
Chasing Justice
Pursuing Justice
Justice - Complete Series

Kissed by Billions
Kissed by Passion
Kissed by Desire
Kissed by Love

Leaning Towards Trouble
Trouble
Discord
Tenacity

Love on the Sea Series
Ships Ahoy
Rough Sea
High Tide

Love You Series
Love Life

Need Love
My Love

Managing the Billionaire
Never Enough
Worth the Cost
Secret Admirers
Chasing Affection
Pressing Romance
Timeless Memories
Managing the Billionaire Box Set Books #1-3

Managing the Bosses Series
The Boss
The Boss Too
Who's the Boss Now
Love the Boss
I Do the Boss
Wife to the Boss
Employed by the Boss
Brother to the Boss
Senior Advisor to the Boss
Forever the Boss
Christmas With the Boss
Billionaire in Control
Billionaire Makes Millions
Billionaire at Work
Precious Little Thing
Priceless Love
Valentine Love

The Cost of Freedom
Trick or Treat
The Night Before Christmas
Gift for the Boss - Novella 3.5
Managing the Bosses Box Set #1-3
Managing the Bosses Novellas

Mislead by the Bad Boy Series
Deceived
Provoked
Betrayed

Model Mayhem Series
Shameless
Modesty
Imperfection

Moment in Time
Highlander's Bride
Victorian Bride
Modern Day Bride
A Royal Bride
Forever the Bride

My Best Friend's Sister
Hometown Calling

A Perfect Moment
Thrown in Together

My Darker Side Series
Darkest Hour
Time to Stop
Against the Light

Neverending Dream Series
Neverending Dream - Part 1
Neverending Dream - Part 2
Neverending Dream - Part 3
Neverending Dream - Part 4
Neverending Dream - Part 5

Outside the Octagon
Submit
Fight
Knockout

Protecting Diana Series
Her Bodyguard
Her Defender
Her Champion
Her Protector
Her Forever

Protecting Layla Series
His Mission
His Objective
His Devotion

Racing Hearts Series
Rush
Pace
Fast

Regency Romance Series
The Duchess Scandal - Part 1
The Duchess Scandal - Part 2

Reverse Harem Series
Primals
Archaic
Unitary

RIP Series
Track the Ripper
Hunt the Ripper
Pursue the Ripper

R&S Rich and Single Series
Alex Reid
Parker

Saving Forever
Saving Forever - Part 1
Saving Forever - Part 2
Saving Forever - Part 3
Saving Forever - Part 4
Saving Forever - Part 5
Saving Forever - Part 6
Saving Forever Part 7
Saving Forever - Part 8
Saving Forever Boxset Books #1-3

Shifting Desires Series
Jungle Heat
Jungle Fever
Jungle Blaze

Sin Series
Payment for Sin
Atonement Within
Declaration of Love

Southern Romance Series
Little Love Affair
Siege of the Heart
Freedom Forever
Soldier's Fortune

Spanked Series
Passion
Playmate
Pleasure

Spelling Love Series
The Author
The Book Boyfriend
The Words of Love

Taboo Wedding Series
He Loves Me Not
With This Ring
Happily Ever After

Tattooist Series
Confession of a Tattooist
Surrender of a Tattooist

Heart of a Tattooist
Hopes & Dreams of a Tattooist

Tennessee Romance
Whisky Lullaby
Whisky Melody
Whisky Harmony

The Bad Boy Alpha Club
Battle Lines - Part 1
Battle Lines

The Brush Of Love Series
Every Night
Every Day
Every Time
Every Way
Every Touch
The Brush of Love Series Box Set Books #1-3

The Debt
The Debt: Part 1 - Damn Horse
The Debt: Complete Collection

The Fire Inside Series
Dare Me
Defy Me
Burn Me

The Gentleman's Club Series
Gambler
Player
Wager

The Golden Mail
Hot Off the Press
Extra! Extra!
Read All About It
Stop the Press
Breaking News
This Just In
The Golden Mail Box Set Books #1-3

The Lucky Billionaire Series
Lucky Break
Streak of Luck
Lucky in Love

The Sound of Breaking Hearts Series
Disruption
Destroy
Devoted

The University of Gatica Series
The Recruiting Trip
Faster
Higher
Stronger
Dominate
No Rush
University of Gatica - The Complete Series

T.N.T. Series
Troubled Nate Thomas - Part 1
Troubled Nate Thomas - Part 2
Troubled Nate Thomas - Part 3

Toxic Touch Series
Noxious
Lethal
Willful
Tainted
Craved

Undercover Series
Perfect For Me
Perfect For You
Perfect For Us

Unknown Identity Series
Unknown
Unpublished
Unexposed
Unsure
Unwritten
Unknown Identity Box Set: Books #1-3

Unlucky Series
Unlucky in Love
UnWanted
UnLoved Forever

War Torn Letters Series
My Sweetheart
My Darling
My Beloved

Wet & Wild Series

Stormy Love
Savage Love
Secure Love

Worth It Series
Worth Billions
Worth Every Cent
Worth More Than Money

You & Me - A Bad Boy Romance
Just Me
Touch Me
Kiss Me

Standalone
Wash
Loving Charity
Summer Lovin'
Love & College
Billionaire Heart
First Love
Frisky and Fun Romance Box Collection
Beating Hades' Bikers

Watch for more at www.lexytimms.com.

Fierce

DARKEST NIGHT #5

USA TODAY BESTSELLING AUTHOR

LEXY TIMMS

In the dark the monsters hide

Copyright 2020

---

1.   http://bookcoverbydesign.co.uk/

Darkest Night Series

Savage

Vicious

Brutal

Sinful

Fierce

Find Lexy Timms:

LEXY TIMMS NEWSLETTER:
http://eepurl.com/9i0vD
Lexy Timms Facebook Page:
https://www.facebook.com/SavingForever
Lexy Timms Website:
http://www.lexytimms.com

Payment
FOR SIN
SIN
LEXY TIMMS
Bestselling Author
Lexy
Timms
FREE
DOWNLOAD

COMING SOON

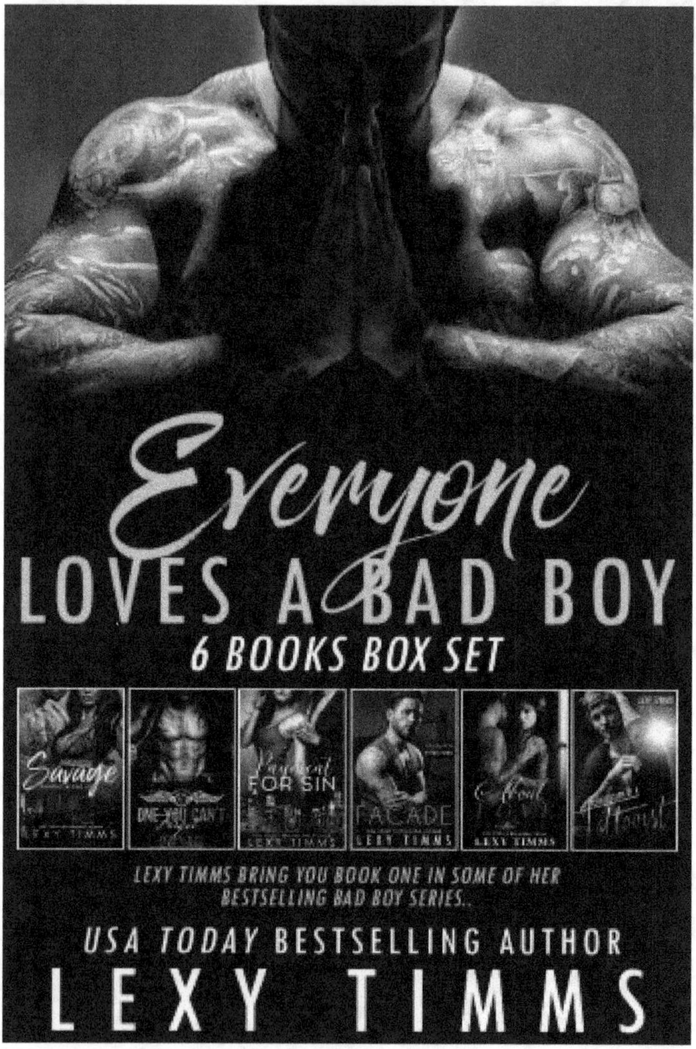
Everyone
LOVES A BAD BOY
6 BOOKS BOX SET
Savage
FOR SIN
FACADE
LEXY TIMMS BRING YOU BOOK ONE IN SOME OF HER
BESTSELLING BAD BOY SERIES..
USA TODAY BESTSELLING AUTHOR
LEXY TIMMS

Want to read more...
For **FREE**?
Sign up for Lexy Timms' newsletter
And she'll send you updates on new releases, ARC copies of books
and a whole lotta fun!
Sign up for news and updates!
http://eepurl.com/9i0vD

Fierce Blurb

PAIN SHAPES A WOMAN into a warrior—into someone fierce...

Fighting for my life against Ransom Tyrell, the only thing that keeps me going is the minute chance that I'll get to see Mia again.

The woman I love is out there, somewhere, and I just have to believe that she's safe. But she's stubborn. And she's not going to give up on me that easily.

Even though I told her to run, she's never been one to play by the rules.

With the help of some old friends and even some enemies - we're going to make a last stand against the man who has stolen everything from her.

Chapter One

Gabriel

I HESITATED OUTSIDE the morgue. I knew I was going to have to tell him, one way or another. But I wasn't sure that Vincenzo was ready to hear what I had to say. Not so soon after he had just seen the bloodied corpse of his own son.

I took a deep breath and pushed open the door. I knew that he must have been exhausted after everything that had happened, but we had to keep pushing. Every second that we were standing here, it was another second Mia was in danger. That she was stuck with that pig. That monster. That man who would rip her apart the first chance he got, just because he liked to watch her bleed.

Vincenzo had come down to the morgue to be with Vinny's body. I knew that he must have been hurting. I couldn't even imagine how much pain he was in. Especially knowing that he was the one who had caused this mess in the first place. If only he hadn't gotten involved with Ransom, none of this would ever had happened, and he knew that, deep down in his bones. He knew that he only had himself to blame, and that must have been the worst part of this.

It was silent in the cold of the morgue—Vinny's body, cleaned, was lying on the table. I eyed him for a moment. I didn't often see bodies after they had been cleaned up, and there was something unsettling about it. Like I was looking at something I shouldn't have ever seen. I didn't like the way he looked: gray, empty, like he had been hollowed out. The life had been torn from him too soon. He hadn't deserved this. He had just been trying to safe his sister, save me. He didn't—he shouldn't...

I had taken so many lives in my life, it seemed odd that this one should make me feel this way. But it was impossible for it not to hurt, at least a little. I had protected this man for so long. He had been one of the only people I could call a friend. He had liked me not only because I had worked for him, but also because he actually thought I was a decent person. Not many people saw that in me. Not many people had reason to.

Vincenzo was shaking as he stood there next to his son's body. I knew that he was hurting right now, but I needed him to snap into work mode. I needed him working at full capacity. He had another child, one who was in the middle of the worst situation she could be in as he stood there. He couldn't risk just doing nothing.

"Vincenzo," I murmured, and he didn't look up. It was like he hadn't even heard me. He was staring at Vinny's body, his brow furrowed, like he could push life back into him if he just looked long enough, tried hard enough.

"Vincenzo," I repeated myself. The mortician was standing to the side, looking grim, as though he wanted to be anywhere other than there right now. I didn't blame him. Vincenzo was hardly a man you wanted to be stuck with at the best of times, and this was far from one of those. He still ignored me. I couldn't deal with it any longer. There would be time to grieve for Vinny when this was all over. However it ended. He hadn't died for us to stand here and fail to save the sister who he had thrown himself in front of a bullet for.

I put a hand on his shoulder, and Vincenzo rounded on me. His eyes were written with anger, and he grabbed my collar.

"You were meant to protect him." He snarled at me. I didn't push him off. No point.

"I haven't worked for you since Mia left," I told him firmly. "But she's my priority now. And she should be yours too. I know that this is going to be hard for you, Vincenzo, trust me, I do. But you have to listen to me. You have to hear me out."

"What is there to say?" he asked, looking back over at Vinny's body. "He's gone. Nothing I do is going to bring him back."

"But you can still bring Mia out of there safely," I explained. "She's at the house now. I just got in touch with Jasmine. She says that Ransom Tyrell has moved in. And he's talking like he owns the place."

"Fucking hell," Vincenzo muttered, rubbing his hands over his face. His eyes were distant, the grief still catching up with him. I didn't want to be there when that bomb went off. But it wasn't like I was going to have much of a choice.

"But that means that we know the ground we're going to be fighting on," I pointed out. "So we have some advantage, right? That's what we have to focus on."

"I don't know how you can talk like this, like it's okay—"

"Because I have to believe it's going to be," I told him at once. "I have to, Vincenzo. And I need you to do the same thing for me. Can you manage that?"

He looked at me again, and he shrugged. He looked younger—not childish, but vulnerable. It was about the first time that I had ever seen an expression like that on his face, and it threw me off a little. I didn't like the look of it, the shape of it. I might have hated him, might have hated the danger that he put Mia in, and might have hated what he had led Vinny into, but he was still a man who I had looked up to for a long time. Giving up on that, seeing it change so suddenly—yeah, I wasn't sure that I could get behind that. It made my stomach churn.

But he was the best bet that I had to make this work. The only way that I was going to be able to save Mia was if he was on my side, no matter how little I knew that he wanted to work with me.

"I need you to think," I told him, trying to keep my voice as calm as possible. I shifted a little on the spot, so that he wouldn't be able to see his son's body like he had before. The last thing I needed was him getting thrown off and forgetting what mattered here. I knew that he had to grieve his boy, but he could do that once he had his girl back.

"What else am I meant to think about?" he asked me, shaking his head. "I can't—"

"There must be other families out there who are willing to work with you against Tyrell," I explained. "He's newer than you. Even if he has the house, you still have some power, don't you?"

"There ... there might be a few," he agreed.

"A few is a start," I replied. "Might be enough. How fast can you put them into action?"

"I don't know," he replied.

"Okay, you have to move as quickly as you can," I told him. "We need to get Mia out of there."

"Mia," he murmured, and it was the first time in a long time since I had heard him say his daughter's name with any sense of love in his voice. It was almost a shock, hearing it like that. I knew that he cared for her, somewhere deep down, but if it had taken the loss of Vinny to work that out, I wondered how much longer it might have taken if he hadn't watched his son die in front of him.

"I know you've lost one child, but you don't have to lose the other one," I told him. "We just have to move fast, before Ransom does something that..."

I trailed off. I didn't need to fill in the blanks for him. He knew Tyrell better than I did. And he knew what he would do to his daughter now that he had her where he wanted her.

"What's the plan?" Vincenzo asked. Okay, now we were getting somewhere. Slowly but surely, he was coming back to his senses.

"I haven't put together anything solid yet," I admitted. "But I have to get to the house, and I think I can provide a distraction long enough for someone else you trust to get in there and pull Mia out."

"You're going to walk in to Tyrell's territory?" he asked, sounding incredulous. "You know that you're going to get yourself killed, don't you?"

I fell silent. If that's what it took to get Mia out of there, then I would do it. In an instant. She needed me right now, maybe more than she had ever needed me before. I had promised her that I wasn't going to stop fighting as long as I still had breath in my body, and I meant that. I had told Jasmine to tell her that I would be there as soon as I could, and I had to follow through on that sooner rather than later. I had to make sure that she kept the faith in me. More than anything, I needed her to be able to trust me at my word. And I wasn't going to give her any reason not to take me as I came.

"If that's what it takes," I replied. "If it gets her out in one piece."

"I'm on the same page as you," he agreed, and he snorted with amusement. It sounded hollow, but it was something, at least.

"I think that's the first time that's happened in a while," he remarked.

I nodded. "Strange bedfellows," I told him. I didn't want to think about how much bad blood there was between us now. More than I had ever believed that there could be. We had worked together for so long, it was strange to think that he hated me as much as he did right now.

He reached up and put his hand on my shoulder. His gaze was steady now, sure, as though he had come to terms with something inside his own head. There was a flicker of my old boss there. At least the promise that he could pull that man out of the mess that he was in. That he could convince people to stand behind him and get ready to fight for his life, for his legacy. For his daughter.

"If you get her out of there," he told me, speaking surely, "all is forgiven."

I looked back down at him. I wasn't going to let him get away with it that easily. He had put Mia through so much, so much that could have been avoided if he had actually listened to his gut instead of going with what he thought he already knew. I hated him, more than I thought I could ever hate someone who had brought me in off the streets, more than I ever believed I would.

But we needed each other right now. And that meant that I was going to have to bite my tongue long enough to get through this mess.

"I don't think that I'm the one who has to ask for forgiveness," I replied, and I shrugged his hand off my shoulder and walked out of the morgue once more.

I could practically feel Mia calling to me. We were so far removed from each other right now, but I would find her. I would find her again, if it was the very last thing on this earth that I did.

And I had no doubt that Ransom Tyrell was going to try his damn hardest to make sure that it was.

Chapter Two

Mia

I GRABBED JASMINE'S hand and pulled her close to me. I wasn't going to let Ransom hurt her. I didn't care what he did to me, but my best friend should never have been pulled into this. And I wasn't going to let her regret this.

"I didn't realize that I was going to get spoiled with a whole other woman tonight, my girl," he murmured to me, his eyes flicking over to Jasmine, sliding up and down her form. "Though, of course, I always welcome anyone else—"

"She's my friend," I told him at once. "She came here to check on me. Since you didn't exactly seem interested in taking care of me."

"Oh, is that so?" he asked, and he narrowed his eyes at Jasmine.

She nodded. "We've been best friends for years," she replied. "Since I started working here. I just wanted to make sure that she was okay. I haven't seen her since..."

"Since I ran away," I finished up bluntly. I knew that she was trying to be careful about what she came out with, but I didn't have any such reservations. I could, at least, say what was on my mind. Ransom might have punished me, but I doubted that it would have been anything more unpleasant than what he would have done if he had been rewarding me, to be honest.

"Ah, yes, I forgot that you had a life here before you pulled your vanishing act," he remarked, a sneer to his voice.

I wanted to spit on his shoes. I hated everything about that man. He liked to think that he understood me, inside and out, that he already had the measure of me, but he didn't have a clue. And I intended to make sure that he knew that.

"I just wanted to make sure that she was okay," Jasmine repeated. She seemed terrified. There was a quiver to her voice, and she was trembling slightly. She had never dealt with someone like Ransom before. She didn't know what he was capable of. But she knew, clear as day, that someone like her was disposable to him, and that he wouldn't pause in making sure that she and everyone else knew that too.

"I haven't eaten all day," I protested. I knew that I needed to get him out of this room as soon as I could. He was going to figure out that I was hiding shit from him, and if Jasmine got caught up in all of this, then she'd have to pay for it too. I didn't want her to have to suffer for my mistakes. She had already done enough of that. In fact, I'd had enough of people paying for what I'd done wrong to last a lifetime. My mind flashed to Kline. Had she been one of them? I had no idea, and it wasn't like I could do anything to find out without implicating her in the mess that I was in the middle of right now.

"And you weren't going to tend to my needs," I continued, trying to keep my voice as neutral as possible. I didn't want him to know that he was managing to get under my skin. He didn't deserve that sort of satisfaction. I knew that it would have delighted him if he'd known that he was succeeding in scaring the shit out of me. He was looking for a chink, an inch of weakness, and as soon as he found it, he was going to exploit it for everything that he was worth.

"Oh, trust me, I have every intention of tending to your needs," he told me, and he looked me up and down like he was already imagining everything that he wanted to do to my body. I shivered. It was hard to fight the hot vomit that rose in my throat when I thought about the danger that I was in, of everything he wanted to do to me, but I had to keep it together.

"But I was too busy making sure that the vomit got cleaned off my shoes properly to worry about that," he continued, his top lip curling with disgust at the memory of it. I had to fight a smirk. Wait until I told Jasmine that I had thrown up all over his precious expensive shoes. She was going to think it was the funniest thing in the world. Anything to get one over on this piece of shit.

"Besides, I thought you would be too … emotional to eat anything," he finished up. I knew what he was trying to say to me. He wanted to starve me out if he could—to prove to me that I couldn't even trust myself, my feelings, my needs. It wouldn't go well, he must have figured, if I had allies in the house. But I had been here longer than he had, and he was going to have to deal with that if he was going to pull through with any kind of victory.

I had to do something to get Jasmine out of here. Every moment that the door was closed and he was in here, it was another second that she risked getting hurt because of his temper. I had seen how he could act when he had decided to push into insanity—when he had pulled the trigger on my brother, on my father. I still didn't even know if they had survived. But at least I knew that Gabe was coming. And that, for the time being, the most important thing was keeping this guy talking, in the hopes that he wouldn't lay a hand on me before the man I loved came to find me once more.

I started swaying on my feet, hoping that I was selling it. It was dramatic, but he didn't seem to be taking the hint. If this was what I had to do, I would do it.

"Mia, are you okay?" Jasmine asked urgently, and I put a hand to my forehead.

"I'm not sure," I replied. Jasmine seemed to catch on at once, and she guided me back toward the bed. I knew that it wouldn't be hard to sell myself as pale, on the brink of passing out, since that's how I had felt since he had put me on that boat in the first place.

"Here, sit down," she murmured, and she put an arm around me. Ransom was still standing there, clearly not buying the story that I was trying to spin. I tried to blur out my eyes, hoping that he would feel sorry for me, and I looked up at him.

"I'm so hungry," I whispered, too dramatic to believe, if it hadn't been for the fact that this guy probably would have brought anything. He sighed and rolled his eyes. He sounded pissed. I just had to keep going a little while longer.

"You need to let me get her something to eat," Jasmine pleaded with him. "Just a sandwich or something. She needs to eat."

He eyed me for another moment. I wasn't sure that he was buying it. I closed my eyes and let out a groan, trying to sell it. I just needed to keep this going a little while longer. And maybe if he thought I was sick, he would be too grossed-out to try whatever it was that he had thought that he wanted to when he walked in here.

"Fine," he snapped. "Go down to the kitchen and make her something quick. Nothing too heavy. I don't want her looking fat in her wedding dress."

A flare of rage hit me, but I couldn't show it. He was probably trying to get me to come out and admit that I wasn't feeling as bad as all that, but I just kept my eyes closed and let my body sink back into the bed behind me.

"I'll be right back," Jasmine told him, though I was sure that she was saying it to me just as much too. "Ten minutes. Tops. Okay?"

"I'm sure we'll find some way to entertain ourselves," he replied, his voice drawling with amusement. It was strange, really, how uninterested he seemed in my consent, in my enjoyment of this. From the very first moment that Gabe had planted his lips on mine, he had wanted to make sure that I was as much a part of this as he was. As though I could ever have denied the intensity of our passion for each other. Nothing could have stopped the way I felt about him. I had never been with another man, but I hoped that I never had to be. Because if Ransom Tyrell was any representation of how they were going to treat me, then it was for the best that I stuck it out with Gabriel above everyone else.

Though it wasn't fair to judge the rest of the men in the world on how this one treated me. He wasn't representative of anyone but himself. Even my father seemed to have more integrity than he did, and I was certain that had to be a first.

Jasmine rose to her feet and headed to the door. She gave me one last look, which was meant to tell me that she would stay if I wanted her to. If I couldn't handle this man, then she had my back.

But I knew that I had to get her out of there. I had already caught her up in more danger than I ever should have. Even just answering that call from Gabriel had probably put her in the firing line, and she didn't even understand just what that meant. She might have heard what Tyrell had been willing to do, but she hadn't seen it—and she would never understand it until she did.

And I'd do everything that I could to protect her from it. I was a different person than I had been when I had first met her. And that person ... that person would never sit back and take everything she had done for me for granted. She had been there for me when I had been sneaking into Gabriel's room, when she knew that being discovered could have ruined her life. Her career. Maybe even more than that.

I widened my eyes at her, telling her that it was safe for her to leave me here. She stepped out of the door, making a point to leave it open.

But Tyrell wasn't going to have that. He moved toward it, then pushed it shut until the room filled with a *click*. It bounced around inside my head, louder than it had ever been before.

He turned back to me. His eyes were dark, and they were full of something worse than anger. Something worse than hate. Something that told me that there was only one thing on his mind, and that he wasn't going to rest until he got it. I had been faking my illness till that moment, but the way he was looking at me now, I suddenly realized that it was as real as it possibly could be. My heart started pounding in my chest, the blood rushing around my ears. I was in fight-or-flight mode. So why did I feel like I was frozen to the spot?

"At last," he murmured, as he unpopped the buttons on the sleeves of his shirt. There was something threatening about the gesture, even though I knew there was nothing about it that should have been.

"I have you all to myself," he finished up. And, as he stood there in front of me, looking down at me, I knew that I didn't have the control of the situation any longer. And I prayed that Jasmine really wasn't going to take any longer than ten minutes. Because I didn't know how much longer I could fight him off.

Chapter Three

Gabriel

"OUT," VINCENZO ORDERED the driver. He looked surprised, but a moment later, he climbed out from behind the wheel of the sedan, and stepped aside so that I could get in.

I knew that we were running out of time. Every second that I wasn't with Mia, it was another when Ransom could have come and taken her for good. And there was no way in hell that I was going to let that happen. I had to move fast. Faster than I had ever moved in my life. And that started now.

But before I went, Vincenzo had something to say to me. I had to fight the urge to brush him off the window, but I knew that he wouldn't have taken that well. He still needed to feel like he were in control here, even if I knew deep down that I was the one in charge.

"Gabriel," he murmured, and I looked over at him.

"What is it?"

"Get him alive," he ordered me. "I want to be able to look him in the eyes when I kill him."

I nodded, much as I would have liked to choke the life out of that Ransom fucker myself, I knew that it was Vincenzo's job. He had taken more from Vincenzo than he had from me after all.

But if I got there and found out that he had done anything to hurt my precious Mia, then I would tear him apart at the seams. And nothing would stop me taking what I wanted so badly.

I wasn't scared, even though I likely should have been. Hard to be scared, when all I could think about was getting out of there and getting to her. I needed her to know that I was coming. I was sure that Jasmine would have passed the news on to her by now, one way or another, but it was just ... it wasn't enough. I wasn't going to feel happy again until I could hold her in my arms. And every second that Vincenzo stayed here talking to me was another that his daughter could have been in more danger than we could get her back from.

"I will," I replied, and he let his head sag for a moment, taking a deep breath.

"And get her out," he warned me.

There was no need to tell me that. I had already dedicated every inch of myself to that task as it was. But if it was what he needed to hear—if it was what he needed to say to me to feel as though he had done enough to rescue his little girl—then so be it.

"I need to go," I told him bluntly. "How fast can you gather people down at the house?"

"I'll move quickly," he promised me. "I don't know exactly how long it's going to take, but I'll make it work, okay?"

"Okay," I replied. For a split second, an inch of doubt flashed through my mind. What if he was lying to me? Was this some game to try and get Mia and me back where they needed us so that we couldn't take off again? But then I thought back to his reaction to his son's body, and I knew that he could never have planned for that. Not in a million years. Not if he had been trying with all his might.

I tore away from the morgue once more. I couldn't wait around a moment longer. I had already been here for far too long as it was, and nothing was going to convince me to stay. I had to get to her. To Mia. She needed me right now, probably more than she had needed me in all the time that we had known each other. And I had to hold her in my arms again, if I was ever going to feel like I was worth anything at all.

The sedan was an ugly thing, but it was fast, and I put the pedal to the metal to get myself across town as quickly as I could. I knew that if the cops pulled me over, I could just point out that I was working with Vincenzo, and they would let me go at once. No need for them to know that I had betrayed him and had stolen his daughter away. Not if I could help it.

The roads were quiet this early in the morning, and I focused on the way that the lines vanished beneath my wheels, over and over again. Okay. I could do this. I could get to the house, and I would find a way to get her out. I didn't know where she was or who she was with, but at least she was in that place—at least I would be working with ground that I was familiar with. Tyrell had probably assumed that we wouldn't dare come fighting for what we were owed, but he had another thing coming. If there was one thing that he should have known about the Romano family—and one thing that I was sure he did know, now that he'd been alone with Mia for a few hours—it was that they were stubborn, and they were reluctant to give up what they knew belonged to them if they could help it.

Good. That's the attitude I needed today. As the car cut through the quiet streets, and I kept an eye out for anyone who might have been looking to take me out if they got the chance, I tried not to think about how easy it would have been for someone to fire off a bullet at me and kill me at the wheel. I was exhausted, and I knew that my usual senses wouldn't be firing on all cylinders as a result. My eyes were beginning to droop, and if I'd had time to stop for a coffee, I would have done just that. But I'd have to survive without the caffeine injection for the time being, and hope that I would be together enough to take on whatever was there for me when I got down to the house.

It was strange, turning down the road toward the mansion once more. Some part of me had sworn that I would never go there again, not after Mia had made her escape a few days before. I had believed that this place would only ever be a prison for her, for us, and that going back would be nothing more than a hopeless defeat.

But I could still change that. She was probably feeling pretty defeated, but I was going to fight with everything that I had to get her out of there. I had no idea how her father was going to handle it once I had broken her loose, once he had dealt with Ransom the way he wanted to—I was doing my best not to think about that, in all honesty, because I got the feeling that it was going to be a huge fucking mess. But I could take that on when I got to it. For now, all that mattered was getting her out, and making sure that Ransom hadn't done anything to hurt her in the meantime.

I pulled the car to a stop around the back of a couple of bushes a few hundred feet from the house. I knew that they would be keeping an eye out for anyone who didn't look right coming by right then, and there was no way that I was going to get away with sneaking up on them in this big fuck-off sedan if they spotted me.

I slipped out of the car, wished that I had a gun on me—I looked through the glove compartment, and, sure enough, there was a box in there that responded to one of the keys that the driver had left in the lock. Inside, there was a loaded gun waiting for me. That was something, right? I tucked it into my pants and climbed out of the car, taking my time, trying not to rush this.

But I could feel her. I could feel how close she was right now. I wanted to just be there beside her. I wanted to tell her that everything was going to be just fine and that all she had to do was stick things out a little longer and we would be able to be together again. I could feel her closeness and it was driving me crazy, every part of me aching for her, the same way that I was sure she was aching for me.

Just a little while longer. Just a little while longer, and I could have her again. That was what I had to keep thinking about.

I ducked around the side of the mansion, pressed against the back wall so I could make my approach without being seen. It was the same wall that I had used to take out a few of Tyrell's men back when they had first made their attack on the house. Well, I still had no proof that they belonged to Tyrell, but I couldn't see anyone else out there who would have wanted to fuck with the Romano family—who would have had the nerve to take them on—and even the passing thought that he might win.

I made it to the front of the house, and peered in to see who was at the cabin at the gate. It could be a make-or-break, depending on who it happened to be. And when I saw who it was, I knew that I was in with an inch of a chance.

Jerry had worked for Vincenzo for a hell of a long time, longer than even I had, and the two of us had been pretty friendly in the time that we worked there. Maybe he would let me in without alerting the main house to the fact that I had arrived. Maybe.

Maybe I would be able to sneak in around the back if I just made sure to keep out of his way. I had no doubt that he would still hold the loyalty to the Romanos that he always had. In fact, it surprised me, to some extent, to see that Tyrell had allowed so many people who had worked for the family he was stealing so blatantly from to keep working at his new home.

But he hadn't done that by mistake. Nothing in his life had been by mistake. Every choice that he had made, everything that he had done, it was because he knew that he could pull it off. Probably because he had gone out of his way to threaten the families of the people that he had invited to stay there. I didn't even want to think what he might have told them to get them to give in to his twisted fucking games—the thought of it was enough to make me feel sick. I might not have liked everyone that I had worked with over the years there, but they didn't deserve to have to deal with a man like Ransom, a man who was going to exploit their deepest and most profoundly held fears to keep them in line.

And what that meant for me was that I was going to have to go it alone. I couldn't expect any of them to play the game with me. I needed to go out and fight on my own terms, and I needed to make sure that nothing was going to get in the way of the assault on the house that I had once called my home.

"Don't worry, Mia," I muttered to nobody in particular. "I'm coming for you."

And I meant it.

Chapter Four

Mia

I WATCHED AS RANSOM stalked his way around my father's room, picking up trinkets, inspecting this and that—most were gifts from the old country, given to my father by other members of the syndicate.

Tyrell didn't seem to have the same respect for them that anyone else did, though. He let a few items slip from his fingers. Picture frames that contained images of my family crashed to the floor, shattering at once. An empty wine bottle from a distillery that was more than a hundred years old. Every time one of my father's things hit the ground with a *thump* or a *crash*, I flinched. This man knew just what he was doing. And he didn't give a damn just how terrified he was making me.

"Please stop," I pleaded with him. I didn't know why I cared so much about my father's things, but, in truth, I just hated the idea of him going through everything that had been part of my life for so long. I just needed a moment's peace. I wanted to believe that this house could go back to normal when all of this was over, and every time he broke something, every time he demolished another one of my father's pieces, it was just a reminder that it wasn't going to be that easy.

He looked over at me, amusement in his eyes. He was clearly enjoying the fact that I was as distressed as I was, and I hated that I had given him the pleasure of showing him my fear and my pain. I was exhausted, but, at the same time, so full of nervous energy that I couldn't have slept even if I wanted to.

"Defiant, aren't you?" he asked me, the words sounding almost mocking coming out of his mouth. I turned away from him for a second.

"I mean, I'm surprised that you care about any of your father's things," he continued, pausing to look at me. "Given that you ran away from him. His most prized possession, it has to be said."

"I'm not his *thing*," I spat back at Tyrell. He grinned. He obviously enjoyed it when I was angry, and it made me even angrier to think that he saw me just the same way that the rest of them did. As nothing more than a doll that could be passed from person to person at will, exploited and used for whatever they decided was best for me.

"Of course you're not," he replied. "You're mine now."

I shivered. And shook my head.

"No, I'm not."

"You know, you're really quite a puzzle to me, Anna-Maria," he remarked.

"I don't care," I spat back at him. "I'm not just some puzzle for you to—"

"You run from your father," he continued, not pausing to let me talk. "And you get as far away from him as you can. You make sure that there is nobody around who would take you back, and then you go to ... who? His right-hand man. I can't imagine all the suitors you must have had over the years, all the people who would have been happy to make you theirs, if they'd had the chance..."

My mind drifted back to Damien and the first time I had gone to one of my father's big events. If that was the sort of person Tyrell was talking about, then could he really be surprised that I hadn't taken them up on their offers? I could still feel his hands on me, gripping into me, like he owned me already and didn't want anyone to be in any doubt of that. It was enough to make me feel sick.

"But you chose to run to Gabriel," he continued.

"I didn't run to him," I replied.

"But you ran *with* him," he corrected himself. It was about the first time that I had heard him acknowledge the fact that he might have been wrong about something, that he had a break in his ability to get everything right. Almost a bit of development, if I thought that he had been capable of it for a second.

"I just can't wrap my head around why you would have done that, given all the men who would have killed or died to be with you, Anna-Maria," he went on, shaking his head. "It just doesn't make sense to me. And yet ... here you are. I know that you would get out of here in an instant if it meant that you could be with that man again."

"In a second." I snarled back at him. I needed this man to know, more than anything else, that I was never going to give in to him. Of everything that he had done to me, everything he had done to my family, he was never going to convince me to be the good little bride that he had clearly thought he was paying for when he had made that deal with my father.

"But why him?" he asked. He seemed genuinely curious. I looked at him again, not sure if he really wanted to hear the answer, but willing to share it with him anyway.

"Because he was the only one who saw my father for the bastard that he was," I told him. Tyrell chuckled with amusement.

"I suppose you're referring to the deal he made with me," he remarked, and I nodded.

"Of course I am," I replied. "No loving father—no decent person—would ever sell their daughter to the likes of you."

"And Gabriel is so much better, is he?" he asked, shaking his head. "Just because he worked for him and changed his mind when the going got tough."

"He's more than that," I replied, and I felt my voice cracking around the edges. I didn't want to show this man weakness, but it wasn't as though I had much of a choice. My body ached for Gabriel's touch, and it wasn't as though I could hide that, no matter how much I wished that I could.

"Oh, is he, now?" Tyrell asked. There was a dark edge to his voice, and I was sure that I could sense an anger rising up in his veins. I wanted to piss him off, some part of me wanted him to hate me. But I knew that it wouldn't have been enough to stop him in his tracks. He had already decided what he was going to take from me, and there wasn't a thing in this world that could have stopped it or slowed it down.

But, as he looked at me, I could see something else in his eyes. Something that spoke to something ... deeper that he felt for me. It wasn't love and it never had been, that much I was sure about—because if he'd had any inch of care for me, he would have let me go as soon as he'd gotten his hands on me.

But this was more than just about owning me. He had been in this room with me alone for what felt like a lifetime now, and if he had wanted to make his move, to hold me down and do what he had been waiting for all this time, then he would have done it. But he was just talking to me. As though he was curious about getting to know me. And no matter how much I tried to push that thought to the back of my mind, I knew that it was true. He wanted something more from me, something better, something deeper. He wanted to make a life with me. Maybe even start a family. He intended to get me to submit to him, to willingly agree that I was going to spend the rest of my days by his side, serving him, giving him everything that he needed.

And that was almost worse than what I had believed before. I could handle him being a monster who wanted to destroy me. But I couldn't handle him being a monster who wanted to love me.

I took a deep breath, then shook my head.

"I think I need to get some rest," I told him.

But he shook his head. "Plenty of time for that later," he replied. "I just want to work you out, Anna-Maria. Daughter of the Romano family, but you have your own ideas for how your life is going to go. Seems more danger than it's worth. Especially getting involved with a man like Gabriel."

He spat his name with disdain, and, for the first time, it hit me that he might actually be ready to tear chunks out of the other man if he got the chance. And not just because he was an enemy, but because I loved him. Ransom didn't want there to be anyone else in the battle for my heart, even if he must have known, somewhere deep down, that I was never going to give it to him, not as long as I lived.

"He's dead," I replied quickly. I had to change tack. Even though it pained me to even say those things out loud about Gabriel, I had to act quickly. I didn't want Tyrell given any reason to go after him, to even think that he were alive. The whole place would be on high alert if they knew that Gabriel had survived that dip into the ocean with my brother and my father, and I didn't want him having to deal with anything more than he already was.

"Do you really believe that?" he asked.

I nodded. "There's no way he could have survived that," I pointed out. "The water was below freezing. He and my father..."

My voice caught in my throat. It wasn't an act. It didn't have to be. The thought of being so alone in the world wasn't hard to be genuinely terrified by. I felt as though I was going to throw up at the very notion of it. Of being so abandoned. Of having nothing ... nothing at all to my name.

But I had to make him believe that. He snorted, though, in disbelief, and I knew that I had failed to get my point across to him.

"Well, much as I'd like to believe that's the case," he remarked. "I don't think that your paramour is quite as easy to get rid of as that. Much as I wish that were the truth that you were telling me."

I fell silent. I didn't know what else to say to him. I wanted him gone, as far from here as he could be, but I didn't know what else I could say or do that was going to convince him to give me the space that I needed so badly right now. He wasn't going to walk out of this room until he was happy in the belief that I was going to give myself to him willingly. And, even though the thought of that was enough to send my panic systems into overdrive, I had to sell that to him, one way or another.

I stared at a spot between my feet on the floor in front of me. And counted down the seconds as I waited for Gabriel to get there. I didn't know how far away he was right now, and I didn't know how much longer I was going to be able to keep this man away from me, but I knew that my chances of getting out of this thing unscathed were counting down with every passing second. And I didn't want to risk anything more than I already had right now.

Chapter Five

Gabriel

I HEADED BACK TO THE car, and started rooting around to find something that would pass for a disguise. I wished that I had thought to throw something in the car that would cover my ass, but I had been in such a rush to get away from Vincenzo that I hadn't been able to think that far ahead.

I knew that someone was going to recognize me if I went straight up to the house without disguising myself. I had to give myself at least a little time before they worked out who the hell I was, and I had to find a way to do that fast. *Hold tight, Mia. I'm coming.*

There wasn't a whole lot in the way of useful shit in the car. The gun was something, but other than that and a few maps, there was next to nothing that was actually going to do much to help me. I started digging under the seats, looking for anything that might have passed for useful—and then it hit me.

In the glove compartment, next to the gun, there had been a few crumpled pieces of fabric. Not much, but enough for me to work with. I opened it again, and sure enough, there was a cap crammed in there, along with some gloves and a tie. Hopefully it would allow me to get up to the main gates without being shot down on the spot. All I needed was to get close enough to allow Jerry to see that it was me, and then I was sure that he would let me in. He had been around since Mia was a little girl, and I didn't doubt that he had as many reservations about her being alone with Tyrell right now as I did.

I threw on the cap and the tie, slipped on the gloves, and made sure that the gun was tucked into my belt deep enough that it wouldn't attract attention. I was still in a lot of pain from the encounter that I'd had with Ransom earlier in the day, but I did my very best not to let it show on my face. I didn't want anyone getting even the vaguest hint of what was going on inside my body. Or inside of my mind. My leg was still aching like a motherfucker, but I had to keep walking like I had somewhere to be.

Because I did.

My pulse was starting to pick up as I approached the main gate. It had been so long since I had been here that I had almost forgotten how imposing this place was. Vincenzo had built it in the style of the old fortresses that had existed back in Italy, where his family was originally from, and that meant that it was set up to act as a perfect base from which to protect yourself against outside attacks. Useful when you were the one on the inside, not so much when you were trying to deal with getting in.

I pulled the cap down low over my eyes. How long would it be before someone clocked that it was me trying to get in? A few minutes? A few seconds? I didn't know if Tyrell had thought far enough ahead to have snipers ready to pick off anyone who dared try to come busting into this place, but it wouldn't have surprised me if he had a few of them lined up and ready to go.

If he hadn't been distracted by Mia, of course.

The thought made my trigger finger itch. I knew that Vincenzo had told me that he wanted Tyrell for himself, but I didn't care. If it came down to it, I would take him out without a second thought, if he had hurt Mia, if he had done anything to her at all...

I reached the front gate, eyes pinned to the ground, and strode toward it. Maybe it would be open. Long shot, but I had to try. I pushed on it, but found it set solid.

"Excuse me!" Jerry's voice called out to me. I ignored him. If I could avoid getting him involved in this, then I would. He didn't deserve to get caught up in the mess that I was about to bring raining down on this house, and if I could have gotten him out of there and been sure that he would be safe, I would have.

"Excuse me," he called again, and this time, I knew that there was no way I could avoid looking at him. With the cap still pulled down, I made my way over to the small cabin that he called his home for the working hours of the day, not taking my eyes off the spot on the ground in front of me. I didn't want him to see me before I was ready. If he was already loyal to Tyrell, then he would sell me out the instant that he laid eyes on me.

"What the fuck do you think you're doing?" he demanded. He sounded on-edge. I had no doubt that he was as thrown as everyone else was by having Tyrell in the house after so long working for Vincenzo. I took a deep breath. If I was going to be able to trade on the relationship that we had, then I needed to look him in the eyes.

"Jerry, it's me." I hissed to him. He didn't reply for a second.

"How the hell do you know my name?" he demanded.

I inhaled again, and tilted the hat back so that he could see who was talking to him. "It's me, Gabriel," I explained, keeping my voice as low as I could so that I didn't tip anyone else off to the fact that I was there.

As soon as he locked eyes on me, his eyes widened. His jaw dropped, and he stared at me for a long moment, as though he couldn't quite believe what he was seeing. I was sure that he thought that he was looking at a dead man right now. News traveled fast among the staff, and, if Jasmine had kept her mouth shut the way she had promised to, everyone would think that I had died out there in the middle of the ocean after Ransom had snatched up Mia.

"Gabe," he murmured. "Is it really you?"

"It really is," I replied. "And I need to get into the house."

He shook his head at once.

"Don't tell me that you're loyal to Tyrell already." I snarled at him.

He shot me a hard look. "Nothing like that," he replied. "But I've seen how many of his men he's already moved in there, Gabe. It's a straight-up fucking army. I wouldn't chance it. You're going to get taken out."

"I have to try," I told him.

He crossed his arms over his chest. "I'm not letting you die for Vincenzo, Gabe," he replied.

I sighed. "This isn't about Vincenzo," I told him. "It's about Mia. It's for her."

He paused for a moment. He must have known that she was in there with him—and he must have known that she didn't want to be. While most of the staff here liked to know little enough to be able to play dumb if the time called for it, he was smarter than that. He always had been. And I knew that he was never going to be the guy who actually believed the bullshit that Tyrell would try to spin about her being there because she just loved him so damn much.

"You're going in to get her?" he asked.

I nodded. "I don't see that I have much of a choice," I replied. "It's—she doesn't want to be there with him, Jerry. And every second that I spend here talking to you is another one that he could be doing something to her that she's never going to recover from."

"Shit," he muttered. "Gabe, you're going to get yourself killed."

"I'd do it myself if I let something happen to her," I told him sharply. He eyed me for a moment. I knew that he would have done anything that he could have to get me to turn around and walk away, but he knew me well enough to understand that it was never going to happen. I needed to get to Mia, and I would take him out on the spot if I thought that he was going to try and get in the way of that happening.

"I'll let you in," he replied, finally, and he looked back up toward the house nervously.

I wondered what Ransom had threatened these people with to get them to do everything that he wanted. I knew that he had to be seriously scaring them if they had been willing to drop the man who they had worked with for so long before he had even been on the scene, and I wished that I could have promised them the same thing in return. Promised that Vincenzo would give them the protection that they were going to feel like they needed to survive the mess that was going to come when we got into that house.

"What can you tell me about how he has it set up in there?" I asked.

He shrugged. "I don't know a whole hell of a lot," he admitted. "But I don't think he's had a lot of time to change everything up since he moved in. He doesn't seem interested in that, at least. I'd imagine that the setup is mostly the same as when you were there."

"Good to know," I replied, and I reached behind me to make sure that my gun was still in place. I needed to be ready with that thing. Fast. No mercy. The thought didn't exactly fill me with joy, but then I remembered what Mia had been willing to do for me when that guy had pulled a gun on me when we had been on the road together. If she could do that for me, something she had never been trained to do, something she had never been prepared for, then I could do this for her. I would do this for her.

"And, Jerry?" I told him. He looked up at me. He seemed wrung out, like he had nothing left to give. He was probably trying to figure out how much danger his family would be in if Ransom found out that he had been cooperating with me, despite the fact that I was persona non grata.

"What?"

"I'm going to need your gun."

"Gabriel, you know I can't give that to you," he protested, but I shook my head. I was going to need all the firearms that I could get. What if the one I had crapped out on me? I couldn't risk it. I didn't have the normal backup that I would have taken into a confrontation like this one. Which meant that I had to provide one on my own.

"I wasn't asking," I replied, and he eyed me for another moment. I knew that he was putting himself on the line for me right now, and I appreciated it more than he could ever know. But he understood that this was for Mia. He had known her long enough, been around this family for enough years to know that she was different. That she didn't deserve this fate. And, though I knew that this was hardly an easy alliance for him to make, he handed me the gun. And I nodded to him in thanks. I was going to make sure that he didn't regret helping me. I was going to make sure that he got his dues for doing what he had to.

Chapter Six

Mia

AS TYRELL CAME TOWARD me, my heart began to pound, even harder than it had before. No. No. No. He needed to get the fuck away from me, but I wasn't sure that there was anything I could do to make that happen.

How long till Jasmine was back? How long had she been away? Being stuck in this room with him, time seemed to pass slower than normal. I knew that it must have been coming up on ten minutes, but maybe she wasn't going to rush back so soon. Maybe she was as scared as she had looked, and she didn't want to put herself in the middle of the mess that I had dragged her all the way the fuck into.

I rose to my feet and headed for the door, walking quickly, not giving him the time to catch up with me. I tried the handle, but it was locked. He must have made sure of that. Didn't want me to get out before he was ready, did he? I wanted to throw up. I could feel that vomit rising again, but I knew that it wasn't going to be enough to get rid of him. If it hadn't before, then nothing was going to change that now.

"Quite the defiant little thing, aren't you?" he remarked, as he made his way toward me, planting his hands on the sides of my shoulders and looking down at me with a beaming grin on his face. He was enjoying this. I wouldn't have been surprised if he got off on how scared I was right now. This was clearly a power thing for him, some enjoyable reminder that he was the one in charge and that nothing that I could do or say was going to change that.

"Get off of me." I hissed to him, and I pushed him in the chest, but he didn't budge an inch. Instead, he leaned down, and rested his nose against my hair so that I could feel his stubbled cheek against my forehead. His closeness was foul to me, almost unholy. I wanted Gabriel to be the only man who had ever touched me, the only man who ever would. I belonged to him in some deep and profound way, and I didn't want a damn thing in the world to change that. I hated Ransom more than I had ever hated anyone before in my life, even my father. Because at least my father had cared for me, somewhere deep down. Tyrell was clearly happy to see me squirm, to watch me as I tried to pull away from him.

He was built solidly, and it wasn't like I could just shove him across the room to get away from him. Maybe the window? But he would grab me before I could get out, and I didn't want to think what he might do to a girl who he saw as disposable. He already had such little respect for me as it was, and making a break for it was hardly going to get him to look at me as anything other than an annoyance who he wanted to make the most of while he still had me.

I tried to scan for anything that could get me away from him. Anything that would give me the space to run. I couldn't stay here for another second. I knew that every moment I passed in his presence was another that he would try and hurt me, try to use me for his own twisted desires. Even if Jasmine came back with the food now, he wouldn't let her in. He was going to see what he could get out of me, and I got the feeling that he wasn't going to settle for what I had given him so far. I wanted him gone. I wanted him dead.

The shock of that thought caught me off guard. I hadn't ever really thought like that about anyone before. Even the man that I had killed, it wasn't like I'd sat back and considered the pros and cons of taking his life before I had pulled the trigger. I hadn't had time for that. I just had to act. But Ransom? Well, Ransom, I had already made my mind up about him. The way he treated me, the way that he talked to me, the way that he seemed to act like he already thought that he had me – my life would be made infinitely better if he wasn't in it.

And so, I had to do something to make that happen.

There was a gun somewhere in this room, I was sure of it. I doubted that Tyrell had thought to sweep the bedrooms for weapons, but he would have been foolish to think that my father wouldn't keep a gun next to his bed. After all, there were men like Ransom out there, looking to take a piece of him whenever they got the chance, and there was no doubt in my mind that he wanted to be ready to take them out at a moment's notice if he needed to.

"What are you thinking about, my pet?" Tyrell murmured to me.

I flinched. I hated hearing him talk to me like that. As though I already belonged to him. If he had known what was really on my mind, maybe then he would have been scared of me. Maybe then, it would have been enough to get him to take me seriously.

But I knew that it would never happen. No matter what I did, I would always be some little girl to him. That was how so many people in this world saw me, as nothing more than an inconvenience to my father and the family at large.

But the question was … could I do it? Could I look into his icy blue eyes and pull the trigger? If I had the choice, would I take the burden of a life on my soul again? I knew now how heavy it was to carry the weight of it with me, and if I could have gone back and told myself just what I would have been facing before, I might not have done what I did.

Ransom deserved it. The world would be a better place if he weren't in it. I had never been so sure of anything in my life before. I could do it if I had to, because I knew that, if I didn't, he would go on causing chaos, making people's lives miserable as much as he could. He would be as hateful, as cruel, he would be as foul to anyone he could get his hands on. If it wasn't me, then it would be someone else.

It might have been Gabriel.

I wondered if he had been able to see through the lies that I had spun to him about Gabriel and the rest of my family being dead. I prayed that he hadn't. I was pretty sure that I was telling the truth about Vinny. There was no way that he could have survived the shot that Ransom had aimed at his chest, the one that he had pulled the trigger on without a second thought.

And if he could kill just like that, then there was no way that I was going to stop myself from doing the same thing. If he thought that he could just rip my family apart like that, as though it were nothing, well, I was going to make sure that he didn't make that same mistake again.

"Nothing," I mumbled, and I tried to duck out from under his arm once more. But he kept himself firmly in place, clearly not quite ready to let me go yet.

"What's the rush, Anna-Maria?" he asked.

I let my eyes slide down to the smashed picture of my family on the ground before us—my brother, my father, and me, back when I had been this gangly, gap-toothed teenager. Back when I had still believed that my father was doing some good in the world, back when I could fool myself that there was still a chance for me to have the life that I wanted to live.

"Please let go of me," I begged him. I wanted him to think that I was pathetic, that I didn't have any way of fighting back against him. Better for him to believe that than to know that I was starting to form the ins and outs of a plan somewhere in the back of my mind. It might have been crazy, but I knew that I had to take the chance. The gun might not even be loaded, and I didn't know if I would be able to get the shots off before he took me out, but it might have been the best chance I had to get out of this in one piece. And to make sure that Gabriel did too.

If I failed ... if I failed, I knew that he was going to kill me. I would be more trouble than I was worth. Unwilling to put out, and unwilling to even just go along with the sick plan that he had decided was just perfect for me. He would kill me without a second thought, and he'd find someone else to use as his bride for this fucked-up empire that he was building.

But being dead was better than standing by and just letting him do whatever he wanted to me. To my family. We had never been the types who would just roll over and let anything happen to us. Vinny hadn't done it, when Tyrell had been trying to take out Gabriel. And I felt like I had to fight, if only to prove that everything that he had done hadn't been for nothing.

"I think that you need to catch up with me, Anna-Maria," he continued, brushing his lips over my cheek. I felt my knees trembling. How could a touch like that feel like such a threat?

Suddenly—a crash. A *huge* crash. Big enough that even Ransom jumped in surprise.

"What the fuck was that?" he demanded, glaring at me for a moment as though I had the answer to that question. Honestly, I might just have, because I had the feeling that it was Gabriel making his attack on the house. And I had the feeling that things were about to get a *hell* of a lot more interesting.

I dived to the window, and gasped when I saw a sedan sticking out of the front of the living room window. The whole building was still shaking from the impact that it had made against the walls, and I could hear chaos downstairs—screaming, panic, everyone freaking the fuck out as they tried to wrap their heads around what had happened.

"What is going on?" Tyrell demanded, but I just grinned at him. For a change, for once, I had the power right now, and there was no way that I was going to let the joy of that slip through my fingers.

Because Gabriel was here. And that meant that it was time to fight. Tyrell was thrown, I could tell that much, he hadn't been expecting an attack so soon, and I was going to use every inch of that to my advantage. I didn't know what we were dealing with, if there would be any other people with him to mount this attack, but he had me inside the house, and I was going to go down there and stand by his side and fight with every inch of power that I had left in my body.

It was what he needed from me right now. What he needed me to do more than anything in the world. And I was going to be sure that I didn't fail him when it mattered the very most.

Chapter Seven

Gabriel

A RINGING IN MY EARS.

The sound of shouting—who was that? Why couldn't I remember? I squinted my eyes, tried to bring myself back into the moment. Where was I? Why did it feel familiar? Why did...?

And then, it hit me.

The car. I had driven the car into the side of the Romano family mansion—and now, I was trying to drag myself back to reality, because if I didn't, they were going to take me out faster than I could blink.

I heard a gunshot fire off, and I ducked down. A second later, a white-hot bullet came tearing through the side of the car and flew over my head. Shit. They were already armed, already fighting back. I reached for the gun in my belt, kicked open the door, and turned to the window. There was a man bearing down on the car fast, but I had managed to knock him back with the door. I fired off two shots at once, and watched as he dropped, heavy, to the ground.

Dust was filling the air. I was pretty sure that the car had crashed into a supporting pillar, and I wasn't sure that it was going to stand for much longer. There was a dump truck of rubble on the hood of the car, and getting out of there in that thing was going to be a nightmare. Right now, though, there was only one thing, one person who I cared about, and I wasn't going to be happy until I could look her in the eye and promise myself that she was going to be okay.

I rolled out of the car, pressing my back against the cool metal and listening to the *hiss* of a popped pipe in the engine. I didn't want to be near that thing much longer, not if I could help it.

My brain started to tune in to the sounds around me. Screaming—the staff probably thought that they were under attack. They were likely already on edge from the fact that Tyrell had walked in there and taken this place as his own with no explanation, but this ... this was a step too far. Most of them didn't have to deal with the horrors of their boss's work up close, but today, all of that was going to change.

There was a rush of them plowing past me right now. Most of them I recognized, but they were hardly making a point to slow down enough that I could get a proper look at them. I didn't care. I wanted as little collateral damage as possible right now. The faster they got the hell out of there, the better.

"Gabe!"

A familiar voice called my name, and my head snapped up. Was it Mia? Could it be? But instead of laying eyes on the one woman that I had been hoping to see, it was Jasmine.

"Get out of here, Jasmine!" I ordered her, as I loaded the gun. I could hear footsteps, and I knew that it wouldn't be long till every man that Tyrell had in his arsenal was out shooting rounds at me.

"Mia," she called to me. "She's upstairs. She's alone. With Tyrell."

"I'm working on it." I growled to her, sneaking a look over the hood of the car to see who was coming at me.

"You can't leave her there any longer—"

"Jasmine, I said I'm working on it!" I told her urgently. I didn't want to be an ass to Mia's best friend, but she was going to be Mia's *dead* best friend unless she got her ass out of there.

"You need to go," I ordered her, jerking my head toward the gash that I had left in the wall.

She shook her head. "I'm not leaving until I know that Mia is out of there."

I sighed. I was glad, honestly, that Mia had someone like Jasmine on her side for all of this, but she was going to get herself in more trouble than it was worth if she wasn't careful.

"I'll get Mia away from Ransom," I promised her. "And I'll send her down to you. But you need to promise me that you're going to get her out of here, all right? Get out, and don't look back."

Jasmine nodded.

"I promise," she swore to me, and I knew she meant it. She'd had a crash course in just how bleak life could be under the rule of a man like Tyrell, and she would have done anything to make sure that she got her best friend away from here in one piece.

"Don't let Mia stop you," I reminded her. "She's going to want to wait for me, but—"

"Don't worry," she promised me. "I'm not going to stick around here for a second longer than I have to."

"Good," I replied, and I cocked the gun. "Now get out. I don't know how much longer this is going to hold. I don't want you here when it caves in."

"But Mia—"

"Jasmine, now!" I ordered her.

Jasmine rose to her feet again, ducked her head down, and sprinted out onto the front lawn to join the rest of the staff, much to my relief. I needed her as far from this mess as she could possibly be. I needed to know that there was somewhere safe for me to send Mia once I had gotten my hands on her again.

Upstairs. She was upstairs, with Ransom, alone. Which meant that the only place I needed to be on the planet right now was there with her. Making sure that the fucker who thought that he owned her understood that he didn't have a single right to her in the world.

There was an explosion of gunfire and another few bullets flew out of the open door, nearly grazing my side. I gathered myself. I didn't have many rounds, and I had no idea how many men I was going to be facing right now. But I needed to believe that I could take them all down. I could. I could. I could do this. I could make it work. If it meant that Mia was going to get out of there in one piece, then I could make it fucking work.

I stood and peered through the dust that had been stirred by the bullets. I had really fucked this place up, and I would have been surprised if it stayed standing much longer. I glanced up. There was a thin crack along the ceiling, a warning sign that it was going to give at any moment.

I heard a cough through the dust, and I spun around to train my gun on the man emerging behind me. I got off two shots and watched the vague shape drop in front of me. Ducking down once more, I crawled across the floor and away from the car as another hail of bullets sailed over the top of me.

My heart was pounding. Blood pumping. All the wounds I had been carrying from getting roughed up on the boat seemed to have gone totally numb. All I could think about was Mia, getting to her, proving that I hadn't been lying when I said that I would do anything that I could to rescue her.

The dust played to my advantage. I held my breath and listened for the sound of men clearing their throats or coughing in the dirty air. It didn't take long till another one revealed himself to me. A cough cut through the air, and I turned to see a man standing in the gaping hole that I had left in the wall. I fired off a shot, but this one was faster and managed to dodge me before he pulled his gun and aimed it in my direction.

"Fuck," I muttered, and I dived to the floor once again, ducking behind the stack of rubble that I had made and glancing over my shoulder. I could hear voices now, clipped, concise, giving orders and taking names. I knew that the rest of Tyrell's army was on their way, and I didn't know if I could take all of them on—

I stopped my thoughts in their tracks. Mia. I had to get to Mia. I didn't care what else happened. I didn't care if they riddled me with bullets. I had to think about her, first and foremost, I had to make it to her, or else I would never forgive myself.

And it was with that in mind that I rose to my feet once more, aimed my gun at the man who had fired at me, and let off two shots, one at his shoulder, the other at his chest. The first landed, sending his gun spinning to the floor toward me, and the second sent him to his knees and then collapsing face-first.

"There, by the car!" a voice declared with confidence.

I scrambled to snatch up the dropped gun and then moved behind a pillar next to the stairs. I glanced up them—if I made a break for it, no doubt they would catch me. It was a wide-open space, and there was next to no cover. I would need to clear out at least a few more of them, stir up some confusion, before I made for the stairs.

I heard a stack of footsteps entering the main hallway, and I pressed my back against the pillar. I didn't know what these motherfuckers were going to be armed with, but I knew that it wasn't going to be pretty. I closed my eyes, caught my breath, and slowed my heartbeat. I couldn't be shaky or slow right now. I had to get past everything that was running through my mind, and fucking do this.

I spun around the pillar, leveled my gun again, and took out the three men who were peering around the car, trying to work out where I was. One of them let out a cry, gurgling with wetness, as the bullet pierced straight through his throat. I dropped down once more, checking the gun, cooling off. I glanced to the stairs once more. *Soon, Mia. Just hold out a little longer.*

"Next to the stairs, come on," another authoritative voice announced, and I hustled to the other side of the staircase. The dust was a little less dense and I could see more clearly, though my eyes were still covered with a film that made everything blurry. I had to focus on my hearing.

Footsteps again. Toward me. I retreated a little farther behind the staircase and peered over once more. Maybe half a dozen men. How many were there in total? I had no idea. Enough that they thought they could take me down. But they had another thing coming. I was doing this for Mia. And nothing was going to stop me.

I pushed the gun through the slats in the handrail, and squeezed the trigger hard, taking out as many as I could at once. There were cries of surprise, a few shots fired off, but the dust was concealing the spark of the gun, hiding me out. I dropped to my haunches again, back against the staircase, breathing hard. I had to swallow to keep from coughing. If they found out where I was, I was as good as dead.

And so was Mia. She was so close to me, and I wasn't going to let her slip through my fingers, not again. If Ransom thought he had won, I was going to correct him as soon as I could. And I couldn't wait to see the look on his face when I told him in person just how much Mia hated his fucking guts.

Chapter Eight

Mia

"FUCKING BITCH!" RANSOM snapped at me, as I dived over the bed and toward the table where I knew the gun was kept. I didn't know if I was going to be able to get the shot off before he grabbed me again, but I had to try. I knew that Gabriel was coming for me, and there was no way that I was going to let him down. I had told him that I would fight, and I had meant every single word of it.

Tyrell grabbed me around the waist just as I reached the bedside table, sending me falling to the ground with a *thump*. I ignored the throb of pain in my knees and pulled open the drawer, yanking out the gun and spinning around to try and fire off a shot. I would kill him. I would kill him right here, and then all of this was going to be over, and I would be free.

But my hand was shaking too much to line up the shot properly, and I cursed to myself as I watched the bullet fly from the gun and up toward the ceiling over his head. A splutter of dust fell from the hole that I had just made, and I went to line it up again, but before I could, Tyrell had dived toward me, pushed me to the ground, and twisted the gun out of my hand.

Straddling me, he kept me pinned to the ground, and a smug smile licked over his face as he eyed me for a moment.

"You know," he murmured, as he brought the gun against my temple. "I think you're going to be a lot of fun."

I wanted to spit in his face, but I knew that any movement could get him to pull that trigger, and I wasn't going to die before I'd had a chance to see Gabe again. The cold barrel of the gun was pressed to my head, and I couldn't help but flinch every time he pushed it a little harder.

But I knew that he wasn't going to kill me. He didn't have it fucking in him. He could have pretended like he had the nerve, but I knew that he would never dare—not before he had gotten me where he wanted me, at least. He was going to make my life utterly miserable if he could, and he wasn't going to let go of me until he was sure that he had broken me, one way or the other.

"Get off me," I snapped, trying to squirm out from underneath him, but he just planted a hand on my shoulder and held me in place. Slowly, he let it travel to my face, skimming his fingers over my skin, making me feel sick.

"Please," I muttered, but I was losing the will to fight him. Which was just what he was hoping for, no doubt. The sooner he broke me, the sooner he would have won, and he knew that he could take me there if he tried hard enough.

No. I would never let him. It didn't matter how hard he tried, how much he cut me off from the rest of the world, from the people who cared for me. I would always love Gabriel. I loved him more than anything in the world, and I wasn't going to let this motherfucker take that from me.

"You can fight all you want, Mia," he murmured, as he twisted my head this way and that. There was a spurt of gunfire below us, and I jumped. Gabriel? Was that Gabriel? Was he all right? I needed to know...

"But I'm sure that you're going to see things the way they are sooner rather than later," he continued, smiling as he pushed his thumb against my closed lips. I twisted my head away from him. Every time he touched me, I felt as though I was going to throw up. I couldn't stand it.

My body didn't feel like mine when I was with him, not the way that it did when I was with Gabriel and I could focus on him, just him. Gabe made me feel as though it was my body and he was just glad to share it with me. Ransom seemed keen to make sure I understood that this was his body, and any connection that I might have had to it would be better off long-forgotten.

"And you're going to love me," he continued.

How could he be so confident? When there was gunfire downstairs? When he knew that Gabriel was going to do anything that he could to get his hands on him? It didn't make sense to me. I had never met a man who was so blind to his own weaknesses. But, I supposed, that was what kept him safe. If he didn't believe that this could be happening, then maybe it wasn't, not in his head. I saw an edge of wildness to his eyes. The same one he'd had when he had pulled the trigger on my brother. This man was truly unhinged. I was lucky to have made it this far without him losing his temper and blowing my brains out.

"I'd rather die," I spat back at him. He pushed the gun harder against my head.

"Careful now," he murmured, shaking his head. "I've been known to make mistakes that I can't take back when I'm aggravated."

My stomach twisted. I almost wanted him to pull the trigger. If it hadn't been for the fact that I knew Gabriel was coming for me, I would have wrapped my hand around that gun and done it myself. I didn't care. I didn't want to live if this was all that I had to look forward to.

And then, suddenly, the door burst open behind us, and a figure threw themselves on top of Ransom, and knocked him back toward the bed.

"Gabe!" I gasped, and he pushed me back against the far wall.

Tyrell tried to level the gun at him, but he fired before he meant to, sending a bullet flying over my head, making me jump. I tucked my knees up against my chest and looked on in wonder as the man I had been dreaming about all this time was really there in front of me. We couldn't have been apart from each other more than a few hours, but still, the sight of him made me feel like I was going to cry with relief. I wanted to wrap my arms around him and just take a moment to tell him how much I missed him, how badly I wanted him. But we had to get out of there first.

"Get the fuck off of me," Tyrell snapped at Gabe, as though he had any right to say anything to him.

I almost laughed. It seemed so ridiculous to me that Tyrell believed for even an instant that he could tell Gabe what to do. Even when my father had thought that he was on his side, Gabriel had worked against him, the way he deserved. I wanted to see Tyrell suffer for everything he had done. And, as he tried to climb to his feet once more, Gabriel grabbed him by the collar and shoved him back against the wall behind him.

Gabe was glaring at him with an unbridled fury that I had never seen from him before. Just the sight of it made me shiver. I wasn't sure if I liked this version of Gabriel as much—or if I just loved him so fiercely that being this close to him was all that I needed.

"You lay a hand on her again, and I'm going to kill you on the spot," Gabe told him, and I hustled my way across the floor and toward the gun that Tyrell had dropped. I knew that we were going to need all the firearms that we could get right now—the heavier armed that we were, the better. I didn't know how many of Tyrell's men were on their way up the stairs right now, but I didn't like our changes.

"Mia!" Gabe yelled to me, a second before the door behind me burst open. He must have heard the footsteps before I did, his ear more finely tuned than mine would ever be.

I managed to fling myself toward his side of the bed before they emerged into the room, and he tucked me under his arm, pulling me closer. I wound my arms around him. I didn't want to let him go. I could still remember the horror of watching him throw himself from the boat and drift off right in front of me. I was never going to let that happen again.

"Get down," he murmured to me, and he pushed me below the line of the bed as he pulled a gun. Two men had entered the room, brandishing weapons. I knew that this was going to be hard to escape. I looked around frantically, wondering if there was some way out of this that I hadn't noticed yet. I needed to flee. I needed to get us out of there. And what about Jasmine? I prayed that she hadn't been hurt in the gunfire that I'd heard below. Or anyone else, for that matter. I couldn't have lived with myself knowing that I had gotten someone hurt, or worse...

Gabe fired off two shots. There was a strike against one of the men who had walked into the room, and it sent him flying back and over the threshold once more. Gabe rose to his feet, leveling his gun at the other one. But before he could fire off, the man pulled the trigger of his own weapon and sent a shot spinning toward Gabe's chest.

"No!" I screamed as soon as the bullet made contact. Gabe hardly seemed to register it, just letting out a grunt as the bullet cut into the spot just below his collarbone. His shoulder jerked backward, but he kept hold of the gun. I scrambled to get to him, but Tyrell was already moving toward me, reaching out to grab me.

"Get your fucking hands off of her." Gabe snarled, and he lunged at Tyrell—and this time, the two of them went staggering back. The glass door that led out to the balcony exploded behind them, and I dived toward Gabriel, trying to get hold of him, to stop him falling over the edge, but it was too late. He and Tyrell, still wrapped up in each other, went plunging over the edge of the balcony.

"No," I whispered quietly, my voice hoarse. I knew that I should have been more aware of the man who was still in the room with me, but he wasn't going to be able to do much until Tyrell gave him another order, and he wasn't going to be able to do that from wherever he had ended up.

I heard a loud splash from down below, and I sank back against the bed once more. I had been so close to Gabe for just a split second, and then he had gone, slipping through my fingers once more. I needed him back. I needed to hold him in my arms, and I needed him to know that I wanted him. That I would do anything to be with him the way that I needed to.

But the fight was far from over yet, and I was scared shitless that we weren't going to be able to win this. But I had promised him that I was going to battle to the end, no matter what happened to him—and I meant that. It was a promise that I was always going to keep.

Chapter Nine

Gabriel

I MANAGED TO PULL MYSELF back up onto the balcony, dripping wet from where I had just crashed into the pool, but Tyrell was quick behind me, and I knew that there wouldn't be much time before he caught up and made sure that neither Mia nor I got out of this place unscathed.

There was a screaming pain in my chest, but I ignored it. There was only one thing on my mind, and that was getting to Mia once more. I could see the fear in her eyes, written all over her face, her body tense and her skin white as a sheet as she tried to understand what was happening. What had Tyrell done to her? Did I even want to know? I got the feeling that finding out was going to make my day a hell of a lot harder—and was going to make showing what little mercy I had left even more impossible.

I cast off the jacket I was wearing, scrambled over the balcony, and through the doors that had been smashed open when Tyrell and I had gone crashing through them. I was a little torn up, but nothing that wouldn't heal. I was more worried about the bullet wound in my chest. I could already feel that grinding sensation, the one that was becoming familiar to me now—blood drooling out of the open wound, time running out. It was a bad one. The guy who had fired it off was clearly a good shot, and I didn't much like my chances against him, especially not in the state that I was in.

"

Tyrell caught his breath on the balcony as I made it over to Mia. She reached for me, winding her arms around me tight.

"Gabe." She breathed. "You're alive."

"Not going anywhere," I promised her, and I planted a kiss on her cheek. Fuck, I loved her so much. I knew that she knew that, but still, if I could have just taken a second right then and there to say it, I might have felt a little better about what I knew that I had to do next—

I felt a hand on my shoulder, yanking me back from her, and I went sprawling across the floor.

The other man who had made the attack on this room.

I had almost forgotten about him. I didn't have a gun. I had lost it in the scrabble. I tried to get to my feet, but he was already on top of me, pushing me back down, jamming his fingers into the oozing wound in my chest, making me cry out in pain.

I pushed my knees into his back, knocking him off of me for a moment, and he fell to the side. I reached for his gun, but he was too quick for that. He brought it around to face me again, and I ducked to the side just in time to dodge the shot he let off. The bang rang in my ears, and I looked over at Mia to make sure she was safe. I knew that this goon wouldn't dare shoot at her. She was far too important to Tyrell, no matter how much he might have liked to pretend otherwise.

Tyrell was likely still catching his breath on the balcony, which meant that I had to deal with this motherfucker, and then I could turn my attention to him—and to getting Mia out of there in one piece.

I managed to kneel on his arm long enough to get his hand to release the grip of the gun that he was hanging on to, and I wrapped my fingers around it. But he had another, and he grabbed for it with his free hand, bringing it up to face me and making me curse with fury. I just needed this guy to stop. I didn't know how much Tyrell was paying them, but it wasn't anywhere near enough compared to the loyalty that they showed to him. He should have been so lucky. What had he threatened them with if they didn't fight for him? Because these weren't the actions of someone who thought they had another option. These were the actions of someone who knew that, if he didn't do as he was told, the people he loved would pay for it.

I dived behind the bed, next to Mia again, and checked the gun once more. Only a couple of shots left in the chamber. I didn't know if I could take him out, but I had to try. I had to give it everything I had right now. She squeezed my good shoulder, and I looked over at her. *For her.* All of this was for her. It always had been, and it always would be.

I rolled out from behind the bed and tried to pull the gun on the man in the doorway. He got off a shot, but it was too fast, panicked, and it flew wide of me, through the smashed hole that I had left in the window. I squeezed the trigger, and, for a split second, was deafened by the sound of the gun as the bullet sped from the hole and toward the man before me.

The sound it made when it hit his skull was deafening, sickening. A wet *thud*. I dropped the gun and dived over to Mia, trying not to let the memory of that awful noise play in my head any longer.

She was shaking, hard. I clasped her face in my hands and looked her up and down. I just wanted to know that she was going to be all right. She didn't seem as though she was dealing with any wounds right now, and I would take that as the blessing that it was. I needed her to be okay. I wasn't going to be able to survive this if she wasn't okay. The damp on my hands was staining her hair, making her shiver even harder, and I kissed her forehead.

"Are you okay?" I asked her, and she nodded.

"I'm okay, Gabe, but you—"

"Did Ransom do anything to you?" I demanded. I could hear the older man groaning out on the balcony and I couldn't help but enjoy the noise. Good. Let him fucking suffer. I wanted him in all the pain that he could possibly be in. He deserved it. If he had laid a hand on her, I would rip them off his body himself. It was the only way I could think to answer him back for everything that he had done to her, to us.

"He didn't," she replied. Whether she was telling the truth or not, I didn't know, but I didn't exactly have time to delve too much deeper into it right now.

"Gabe, you're bleeding," she told me bluntly, and she reached up to touch my shoulder. I looked down at it. I had hardly noticed the pain, but now that she pointed it out, it started to sear painfully once more.

"I'll be all right," I told her at once. "I've survived worse, you know that."

"We can't keep letting this happen to you." She breathed, and I shook my head.

"We're not going to," I replied, and as I looked at her, I knew that I was going to have to do something that she wasn't going to like. Even if it was for her own good, she was going to fight me on this. I grimaced. Right now, I couldn't think of any other way to handle it.

"We need to get out of here," she told me urgently. "I don't know … I don't know how long we've got before Tyrell sends more men up. Gabriel, can you walk? Can you hear me?"

I had drifted off for a moment as I tried to figure out what I needed to do next. It wasn't going to be pretty, but it was what we needed right now. I knew that she was going to fight me tooth and nail, to try and get me to come out of there with her, but right now, we had to work with what we had.

"I love you," I told her, and she looked at me, her eyes wide.

"I love you too," she replied, but she must have known that there was something else just around the corner. I felt awful for what I had to do, but I didn't see any other way to handle this, to handle the mess that was currently running through my head.

"I need you to listen to me," I told her seriously, keeping my voice low, speaking as quickly as I could.

"I'm listening..."

"Jasmine is waiting for you," I explained to her. "She's going to get you out of here as soon as you find her. She'll be waiting near the front of the house, you just have to go find her. Okay? You understand?"

Her eyes glazed with terror and sadness. She knew what I was telling her. That I wasn't going to be able to go with her. I didn't want to slow her down, and I knew that I would be a more obvious target than two girls together.

"I can't go without you," she replied, clasping my hand in hers for a moment. "I can't—Gabe, I won't leave you here."

I eyed her for a moment. I had to act fast. It wouldn't be long until another stream of men burst into this place, and, when that happened, there was going to be less of a chance than ever to get her out in one piece. I wasn't going to risk that. I needed her as far from here as she could possibly be, even if it meant being far from me.

Even if the thought of that was enough to make my skin crawl. I had to put the selfishness to the back of my mind and get the fuck out of here. I could catch up with her later, I would find her again, I was sure of it. I just needed to make sure that she wasn't around when they came back for round two.

"You're going to have to forgive me," I murmured to her, and I leaned my forehead against hers for a moment. She clasped hold of me tight. She must have known what was coming. Or maybe she had no idea, and when I scooped her up into my arms, it took her totally by surprise.

"Gabe!" she exclaimed, but she hung on to me anyway. I needed her to trust me right now, more than she had ever trusted me before. I wanted to hold her there for another second, but I knew that I couldn't. I had to get her out of there.

I strode over to the balcony, toward the pool, and judged the drop—a dozen feet, not far. The pool was deep enough to catch her weight.

"I love you," I murmured to her again. And, with that, I tossed her over the edge of the balcony.

Tyrell let out a howl like a wounded dog and scrambled to try and catch her before she went over the edge, but she was gone before he got the chance, thank fuck. She landed with a loud *splash* in the water below. I saw her flailing for a moment before she managed to gather herself, and I tore my gaze away from her.

I had other things to deal with now. I just had to hope that her best friend was really there for her, ready to get out of this place and get her to safety. But for this instant, I just had to give her a straight run to freedom. And I was going to do everything I could to make sure that happened.

Chapter Ten

Mia

I SURFACED ABOVE THE frigidly cold water of the pool, gasping for breath, and tried to arrange my thoughts. Hard, when the freezing cold was beginning to seep into my veins and pull me back down to the bottom.

"Anna-Maria! "

I looked up. There was only one person who called me by that name. And, sure enough, there he was—Ransom, looking down at me from the balcony. His eyes were narrow, and he looked furious. Good. I knew if he was angry, then something had gone seriously wrong for him, and that's just the way I wanted it.

"Don't move a muscle." He snarled at me as I dragged myself to the edge of the pool, clasping on to the side and shivering helplessly. It was March in Chicago, after all, of course it was fucking cold.

"Anna-Maria!" he bellowed at me again, but I didn't pay him an inch of mind. I didn't care what he had to say to me. I didn't care what he thought he had to do. I was going to get out of there. With Gabriel.

And then, as my thoughts began to clear, I remembered everything that he had said to me. That he had asked me to do everything that I could to get out. I knew that he had gotten himself out of some seriously sticky situations in the past, and now, he was relying on me to do the same thing. I had to believe that he would find a way to get out of there in one piece. I had to believe it, because the alternative was too horrible to consider.

I knew that I was only going to put him in more danger sticking around here. I needed to get the fuck up and get the fuck out before Ransom's men got their hands on me once more, and that meant moving fast, no sitting around and hoping that Gabe was going to emerge from the balcony and come join me. Even though I'd only just found him again, I had to break free. I knew that. I knew that I owed him that.

Jasmine. He'd said something about Jasmine. She had to be waiting somewhere around here, right? I looked around. My teeth were chattering so hard that it was tough to get a clear view of anything, but I forced myself to clench my jaw and focused on the ground in front of me. I heard Tyrell let out a furious grunt from above me. Hopefully, if his attention was trained on how badly I was pissing him off right now, he wouldn't be focusing on Gabriel.

I sprinted around the side of the house, but, before I could get very far, I heard his voice slice through my head again.

"After her!" he ordered.

Okay, now this was serious. Now, I was going to have to run for my life. I turned a corner at the edge of the building, and almost crashed straight into the car that Gabriel had driven into the side of my father's mansion. I was sure that my dad would be pissed about that when he saw it—if he saw it. But, if the house never came back to the Romanos, where it belonged, at least we could be certain that we had caused some serious repairs to be required before Tyrell could move in for good.

I could hear a flurry of activity inside the house, even as I kept my eyes focused forward. My legs were moving fast, even though they were basically numb. I had to keep going. I had to keep moving. Gabriel needed that from me, more than anything.

As I turned another corner to get away from the men who were after me, I couldn't help but wonder if Gabe was still alive. Had Tyrell tossed his corpse over the side of the building as soon as I had gotten away from him? No, I was sure that he would have told me if he had. He would have wanted me to know that. He knew that it would have slowed me down, even if I would have hated it. He knew that losing the man I loved might be the only reason for me to stop running. He didn't know the agreement that I had made with Gabriel, to do everything that I could to get out of there no matter what came next. No matter what happened.

My breath was tearing out of my lungs as I paused to look around the back area of the mansion. The garden had never been my favorite place, but right now, I wished that I had thought to spend more time there. I didn't know where I was supposed to go. And then, I spotted a small path that led down to the back of the house, to a gate that was propped open, and I took off down it at once. I prayed that Jasmine had been able to get out of there in one piece. I couldn't stand to lose anyone else, to live with the guilt of knowing that if I hadn't been who I was, the people I cared about might have been safe.

I heard footsteps behind me, and I dived behind one of the thick bushes that lined the outside of the garden. I had to catch my breath. I knew that I couldn't keep running. My muscles were beginning to seize up from the cold, and if I tried to keep pushing myself, my legs were going to give out right from underneath me. I pressed my lips together to keep from making a sound as I stood there, and watched a couple of the men continue down the path toward the open door. Shit. If Jasmine really was there, then she was in some serious trouble. If they saw her there, waiting for me, it wouldn't take them long to work out that she was on my side and working with Gabriel and me. And that was the very last thing I needed right now.

Fuck. I needed to do something to draw their attention. I racked my brains. A noise? A noise would be enough. I looked down to my feet and picked up the heaviest rock that I could see there, weighing it in my hand for a moment before I threw it with all my might back at the house. It struck the window to my father's office, didn't break it, but made a loud enough *bang* that the guys who had been shooting past me turned at once.

"Did you hear that—"

"It was from back at the house!" the other one exclaimed, and they made their way back past my hiding spot. I held my breath until I was sure they were gone, and then dived out to hit the path once more. My legs seemed to be moving on autopilot, but I didn't care. I could rest when I was out of here. When I was as far from the place that I'd used to call home as I could possibly be. I wasn't going to let myself get trapped here. I wasn't going to let Gabe down, not after everything that he had done for me.

I wished that I had a gun. Something to protect myself. Even though I knew that it would have been hell to pull the trigger again, I would have done it, if it meant that I could run from here and know that nobody would be coming after me. My foot caught on one of the slats of the path and I almost went over, and I had to grab one of the bushes beside me to keep from tumbling to the ground. I knew that if I fell, I wouldn't be able to hide from them any longer. I needed to get as far away as I could manage before they realized that I was gone. Ransom would send this whole city after me if he got the chance, and I needed to do everything I could to prove that I was more trouble than I was worth.

I finally reached the bottom of the path and dived through the small door that led outside. I didn't even know for sure that she was going to be there, waiting for me—just a hunch, a guess, anything that would get me out of this place once and for all. But, as I staggered out of the garden, I saw a small blue coupe waiting for me – and, inside, my best friend.

Jasmine leaped out of the car, then caught me in her arms. My legs were shaking so hard from the cold I could hardly stand any more.

"Get in!" she ordered me, and she pulled open the back door and pushed me inside. I heard voices from back at the house, and I knew that it wouldn't be long until they worked out where we had gone.

"The door, close the door." I gasped to her, pointing toward the still open entrance that led back to the garden. If we could throw them off the scent, even just for a few more seconds, it could make the difference between getting out of here alive or—

She slammed the gate shut and dived back into the car as I tried to buckle myself in. She blasted the heaters and then turned around to look at me with concern in her eyes. My clothes were heavy with water, still clinging to me, and my hair was slicked back from my face. I felt like a skinned rat—naked and exposed.

"Are you hurt?" Jasmine asked me with concern. My eye was drawn, for a moment, to the dream catcher that hung from the rearview mirror. I would never have pegged Jasmine for collecting stuff like that. But then, I supposed, there was so much I didn't know about her, because my interactions with her had always been held back by my father, making sure that I didn't spend too much time with the staff. I couldn't help but smile. Now that I was free of him, of all of this, I was going to get to know everyone who had helped me. Everyone who had saved my life. I shook my head.

"Just cold," I assured her. "We need to get out of here."

"What about Gabriel?" she asked.

I shook my head. "He can handle himself," I promised her. I knew that it sounded cold, but it was what he would have wanted me to say to her. We had to get out of here. I knew that every second we spent outside this house was another second that those men could find us, and if they did, they would kill Jasmine on the spot for trying to help me.

I looked down at my hands. The water had washed Gabriel's blood from my skin, but it was still crusted under my nails. I tried not to let it turn my stomach.

"We need to go," I told Jasmine again. I was certain that this little thing didn't have the same horsepower as the vehicles that would be after us, which meant that our only chance to get away was to make sure that they didn't see us in the first place.

Jasmine finally pulled away from the house and started down a side street. I leaned back and closed my eyes, praying to whoever might have been listening at that moment that Gabe was going to get out of there okay. He had done too much, come too far for him to fail now. And I wasn't going to let him slip through my fingers. Not after everything that we had been through. I needed to know that he was going to make it out of there in one piece. But right now, I had to focus on Jasmine and me making it as far from this place as we possibly could.

Chapter Eleven

Gabriel

I WATCHED AS MIA DRAGGED herself to the side of the pool and heaved her dripping body out of the water. She was shivering hard, but she was still moving, and that was all that mattered.

Ransom was yelling something down at her from the balcony, and I pulled myself back toward the house. The cold air was biting at my skin. I needed to rest. I knew that my body couldn't take much more before it was just going to give in for good, and I wasn't sure how much more I could push it before it just collapsed under me from the weight of everything I had put it through.

Mia was out of there. That was all that I was focused on right now. I knew that Jasmine would come through to keep her safe, I was sure of it. And now that I knew that she was okay, I just had to find some way to get my own ass out of this place and after her.

But Ransom wasn't going to make that easy for me, I was sure of it. I had caused him enough problems that he was going to make sure that he made an example of me. If he could take me out, then nobody would try to fuck with him again, and he had to know that.

The door to the bedroom crashed in once more and I cocked my gun. I knew that I was going to have to fight my way out of there. I had no idea what I was going to do by the time that I actually had to get out—the car that was lodged in the side of the building was hardly going to work for me, and Jasmine and Mia would be long gone if they had actually listened to what I had asked of them. I needed to hold myself together. I could figure out what came next when the time came. For now, I just had to keep my eyes pinned forward. And for the time being, that meant watching the five men who had just burst into the room.

I pressed my back against the bed for cover, keeping my head low. Tyrell was still standing on the edge of the balcony, watching Mia. As I heard the footsteps filling the room, I knew I had to take advantage of the moment of surprise that I had right now, and I spun around from the bottom of the bed and let off three shots in a row.

I heard two loud *thumps* as a couple of the men hit the floor. That was something. I wasn't sure that it was enough, though. I didn't know how many rounds I had left in this gun, and there was no telling how long it was going to take before more men arrived. I knew that Tyrell would have sent a few after Mia, but honestly, I would have much preferred them to come after me instead. I knew that I could take them on. I knew that I could fight for myself. I knew that there was actually a chance in hell of getting her out of there if I could just keep them busy and focused on me and only me.

Even if I didn't know how long I could do that before they would just take me out.

I loaded the gun once more, cocked it, and spun around the bed, my eyes blurring around the edges as I got off another shot. One more man hit the ground—three down, two to go. But as I tried to cock the gun once more, it spluttered water at me and told me that it wasn't going to take anything more than it already had. I dropped it and rose to my feet—no point pretending that they didn't know who they were dealing with now.

One of the guys lunged at me and sent me crashing through the open door and on to the balcony below. The landing knocked all the air out of me. I was soaked from the dip in the pool earlier, and I didn't even know if I could keep myself upright with all these heavy clothes weighing me down. I swung a punch at the guy on top of me and managed to send him sprawling to the ground, but he was replaced by his companion, who was quick to plant a knee in my chest to keep me where I was and stop me from getting the solid breaths I needed to fight.

I shifted underneath him, managing to send him toppling off of me, and then I scrabbled toward the door. I didn't know how many men there might be waiting for me right now, but I had to keep moving. I had to keep going. I had to try and get as far from Ransom as I could. He was going to bring the weight of the world down on my shoulders if he got the chance. As far as he was concerned, I had spoiled the prize that he had paid so much for, and he needed to be certain that I was never going to get close to Mia, ever again. Even if she wanted me to. Even if she loved me.

I tried to get to my feet, but they were weak and my body was starting to give out. I could see dark clouds blurring the edges of my vision, and I tried to stand once more, but my body was not having it. The pain was too intense. The exhaustion—after everything that had happened, my muscles were screaming at me to stop, to rest. There wasn't much more I could take. If it came down to hand-to-hand shit, I was fucked, because I didn't have the strength in me to fight right now. I had nothing left.

I thought of Mia. Mia, the girl who I was doing this all for. Mia, who was probably scared for her life as she sped through Chicago with her best friend, praying that the two of them weren't going to get found and hurt or worse by Tyrell and his men. I needed to do this for her. I needed to keep going for her.

I pulled myself back up on the doorframe, and, as soon as I had, I felt a weight hit me from behind. My body hit the ground once more, my chin bouncing off the hardwood floor, and I groaned in agony. My head was spinning. I couldn't keep doing this. If I tried to keep pushing on, if I tried to keep making this happen, I was going to kill myself in the process.

I turned over, lifting my fists to try and battle the man who had taken me down, and I managed to land a couple of solid blows before he drove one against my jaw and sent stars spiraling through my vision. I groaned again, the pain starting through me like a bullet wound. I couldn't see straight. If I tried to stand now, I would go straight back to the floor. I was fucked. The best I could do was hope that Ransom decided to give me a speech before he took me out, allowing me some time to recover before I got up and started fighting him again.

"Leave him alive," his voice cut through the fog in my head. "Don't touch him. He's done."

I closed my eyes and let my head sink back against the floor. It was almost a relief, though I knew that I was far from safe in that moment. I didn't have to fight, just for one second, and after everything I had been through, I would take it, no matter how dangerous it might have been to trust my safety to Ransom Tyrell right now.

I lay there as I heard footsteps moving toward me. Ransom. I was sure of it. The weight of the man who had been on top of me receded, and I tried to prop myself up against the bed behind me. I became aware of a presence in front of me, and I managed to peel my eyes open long enough to see that Ransom was there, glaring at me with a smile on his face. The mixture was enough to make my stomach curdle, and I knew that he wasn't going to make this easy for me.

"Well, it's good to see you again, Gabriel," he murmured at me, his eyes ice-cold as he looked into mine. "I thought that we might have been friends once, you know. You could have looked after Mia when she was my wife. Given that all you're good for is hired muscle, it seemed only fair that I keep you employed."

"I'll never work for you," I snapped back at him, and he grinned. My vision was so blurry that it looked as though three of him were smiling at me at once. A Cheshire-cat grin, that of a man who knew that he had managed to get everything that he wanted and didn't care who knew it.

"I think you might," he replied, calmly, and he reached out to grip my face in his hand, making me look at him. I wished that I had the energy to spit in his face right now. It was better than he deserved, though.

"I'll make some money off you, at least," he remarked, as he rose to his feet once more. "I can think of a whole lot of people in this city who would be glad to get their hands on you. Who'd probably pay good money for some one-on-one time with you, Gabriel. How do you like that?"

I didn't reply. I couldn't. My brain felt as though it was shutting down. I had fought so hard for so long, and now I was here, trapped with the very last man on earth that I wanted to be anywhere near. And he was going to do everything he possibly could to make my life a living hell. I wanted to rip him apart at the seams, but with the energy that I was handling right now, I was struggling to keep my eyes open long enough to look at him.

"Take him out of here." Ransom ordered to whoever was listening. I had taken out a few of his men, I was sure of that, and had made his life a hell of a lot harder in the process. Good. I wanted him to know how it felt to struggle. And I wanted him to know that, no matter how well he thought he had done, no matter how powerful he might have liked to see himself as, that Mia had managed to get away from him again. He could do whatever he wanted to me, and nothing would stop that being true. The pain was bad, but it was soothed by the sureness that he must have been going nuts at the thought of having lost her yet again.

And it wasn't much. But right now, I would take anything that I could get. I needed to cling to something, something that would make all of this worthwhile, and right now, as I felt arms dragging me to my feet, I clung to that. Mia was out of here, once again, and I had been the one to keep her safe. And that, for the time being, there was nothing that Ransom could do to undo that truth. I had gotten her free. And I would do everything I could to make sure that nothing changed that.

Chapter Twelve

Mia

"WHEN CAN WE STOP DRIVING?" Jasmine asked me. Her voice was taut, scared, but I ignored it.

"When I'm sure nobody is following us," I promised her. I knew that she was terrified, but I had to keep my wits about me. Anyone could have been on our tail right now, and I didn't want to fuck up after Gabriel had put so much on the line to get us out of there.

I remembered what he had done the day that we had been attacked at the coffee shop. He had looped the city a few times until he was certain that we weren't being followed. I had no idea how long it would be before I actually believed it.

We had been driving for at least an hour, but I wasn't going to go to our next stop until I was sure that we weren't being followed. I had been directing Jasmine around the city, keeping a close eye on the rearview mirror and trying to do everything I could to calm my nerves as I focused on what was to come next. I was still shivering, but it had nothing to do with the icy cold that had penetrated my body as I had dried off from the water that had drenched me when I had been dropped into that pool.

"How long is that going to take?" Jasmine asked. Her voice was clipped. She must have been scared shitless. I hated that I had done this to her. Hated that I had let her get so scared, hated that I had allowed her to get caught up in this. She had only wanted to be my friend, and now she was stuck in the middle of this wreck, stuck in the middle of being certain that she wasn't going to make it out alive. She could have run a long time ago, but she didn't. She just kept sticking around for me, waiting it out for me. She didn't slow down, she didn't stop, she didn't give up on me, even when I was sure that the rest of the world would have done just that.

"Okay, I think that we can start heading over now," I told her, once I was certain that nobody was actually following us.

"And where are we going?" she asked me. I took a deep breath.

"Somewhere safe," I promised her. "Okay, take the next turn off of that exit..."

I gave her the directions as we went, and I tried not to let the fear show in my voice. I knew that I needed to keep my shit together for Jasmine, if nothing else. She had already put so much on the line for me, and I needed to pull through and do it for her. I needed to prove to her that she hadn't made a horrible mistake doing this for me.

And besides, I knew that as soon as we got where we were going, she was going to be glad to be out of that house. I knew that she hadn't even really wanted to work for my father, not really, but she hadn't had much of a choice. It wasn't as though there were many jobs that came with room and board in this city that paid as much as the Romanos did, and, when she had to support her family on top of all of that, she needed to make as much as she could in as short a time as possible. I didn't blame her for taking it. I just had to prove that it wasn't going to ruin her life.

Finally, we came to a small spot outside the city, in the suburbs. A house that was warmly familiar to me by now. I wished that we hadn't left it in the first place. I knew that it was probably a crazy idea, coming back here, but I didn't know where else we could go. Kline was the only person in this city, apart from Gabe and Jasmine, who I actually trusted, and I didn't know what else I could do to make sure that my best friend stayed safe in the face of all of this.

"What is this place?" Jasmine asked, as she pulled the car to a halt and sat there in the driver's seat.

"It's safe," I assured her, and, as I climbed out of the car, I heard a chorus of dogs barking. Letting us know that we were welcome here, even if Jasmine didn't seem confident in believing that quite yet.

"Are you sure?" she asked, and I nodded as I pulled open her door.

"I wouldn't have brought you here if I wasn't totally certain," I promised. And I meant it. She had put enough on the line for me as it was, and there was no chance in hell that I was going to let her go through anything more dangerous.

"Right," she muttered, but she didn't sound totally convinced. Still, she got out of the car. The dogs continued to bark, and I heard Kline calling to them, probably telling them to shut up and that she was going to check on it.

I headed over to the door, and Jasmine followed behind me, her car keys clamped tightly in her hand as though she might need to lash out at someone at any moment. I knew that she had every right to be scared, but I just hoped that all of this was going to be okay. I needed Kline to help us right now. She had told me that if I needed her, I could come back, but I didn't know if that worked the same way if I didn't have Gabriel there by my side.

I stood in front of the door, and was about to lift my hand to knock when it sprang open. And there she was—the woman who I hoped was going to come through for me all over again.

Her eyes widened as soon as she set them on me.

"What the fuck are you doing here?" she demanded. Even though she sounded borderline pissed to see me, it was still a relief to hear her voice. I had no idea how much I had missed her until that moment.

"Can we come in?" I asked. She looked past me, to Jasmine, and must have seen the fear on her face.

"Of course you can," she replied, and she stepped aside, pushing a couple of her dogs out of the way so that the two of us could come into her house. She eyed the driveway for a moment, looking up and down the street, no doubt fearful that we had brought a flood of bad news with us when we had turned up.

"What the hell are you doing here, Mia?" she asked me once again as soon as the door was shut behind us. "I thought you were supposed to be halfway to fuck-knows-where by now."

"We were," I admitted. "But they—someone must have told Tyrell that we were on the boat. They found us."

"Shit," Kline muttered, rubbing a hand over her short hair and narrowing her eyes as though she was trying to work out who might have done such a thing. I didn't have any clue who had sold us out, but frankly, at that point, I didn't care. I was just exhausted. I had been through enough these last few days to last me several lifetimes, and I intended to do whatever I could to earn some rest. For both me and Jasmine.

"So your father found you?" she asked. I shook my head.

"It's ... complicated," I admitted. "It wasn't just my father who found us. The man he sold me to? He was the one who came after us. I don't think he had any intention of letting me get out of there with my family..."

I suddenly remembered my brother. I had been so caught up in everything that had happened that I had almost forgotten the pain of watching him pitch over the side of the boat. Knowing that he was gone. I didn't even want to imagine how much he had suffered in his last moments, how much he had been scared shitless that he was going die. And that he had done it for me. He had done it because he didn't want me to lose Gabriel on top of everything else that had already slipped through my fingers.

I sank back against the wall and then down to my haunches, a wave of sickness hitting me hard. I didn't know how I was going to be able to keep going after all of this, after everything that I had been through. I needed to ... I needed to stop. I needed to slow things down. I needed to rewind, to take back what had happened before, and do everything that I could to fix it. It might have been scary, but there was no way that I could move forward knowing what I had been responsible for...

"Mia," Jasmine murmured, and she crouched down in front of me. "Mia, are you still with us?"

"She's in shock," Kline announced. I could hear her voice as though it was coming from a million miles away. There was no way that this could be real. I couldn't have lost so much in such a short period of time. Just a few months ago, I had been living my life, sure that the only thing I would ever have to do was prove to my father that I was capable of taking on everything that this family needed from me. And now...

And now, my world was coming apart at the seams. I had lost so much. I didn't even know if the man I loved, the man who had been at the center of all of this, was alive anymore. And if he was gone, too, I didn't know what I was going to do to come out the other side in one piece. I knew that I had promised him that I would keep going no matter what, but how could I do that when I knew that the only thing that kept my feet moving underneath me was the promise that, one day, I would end up with him in the midst of all of this?

They pulled me over to the couch, and Kline sat down opposite me. Her face was drawn, dark circles under her eyes. I wondered if she had been struggling to sleep since we had gone, worried that we weren't going to make it out of there in one piece. Well, she had been right. I hated it, but she had been right. And I was never going to forgive myself if I had just led another stack of trouble to her door, to boot.

"Mia, you need to tell me something," she ordered me, her voice tense, harsh. It wasn't a tone that I had heard from her before, and I forced myself to look up into her eyes.

"What is it?"

"Gabriel." She breathed. Even just the sound of his name was enough to make me feel as though I had been struck across the face.

"Is he alive?" she demanded. And, as she said the words out loud, I heard a crack in her voice, and I knew ... I knew that she was as scared as I was that we had lost him. I felt my face crumple and I shook my head, no idea what to tell her, no idea what to say. I didn't know if he would ever walk through those doors to find us again. I didn't know if I would ever get a chance to see him once more.

But I knew that I would fight with everything I had to make that happen. No matter what it took from me. Because it was what he would have done for me. And it was the very least I could do in return.

Chapter Thirteen

Gabriel

WHEN I CAME TO, THE first thing I tasted was blood.

I pressed my lips together. My tongue was so dry I could hardly move it around my mouth, but I could taste the dried blood on the inside of my lips. I didn't know how long I'd been out for, but that metallic, gory sensation in my mouth was enough to make me feel sick.

I managed to peel my eyes open, even though they hurt terribly. My entire head was throbbing as though I have been pushed through a meat grinder, and I found myself straining to remember everything that had happened to lead to this moment.

I remembered Tyrell. That's all that I really needed to remember, if I was being honest with myself. I was sure that he was the one who had put me here. I looked at the ceiling above me, and I recognized it as some part of the Romano house, even if I couldn't tell where it was, exactly. My head was too fucked up for that right now. But at least I was still somewhere that I remembered. So that had to count for something.

I went to brush my hair back from my head, but I found my hands bound down to my sides. Shit. So they had made sure that there was no way that I could go anywhere. There was a burning pain in my arm, where Mia had tried to stitch up the wound before. I didn't know how long the pain had been there or how long it would stick around before it went away again. Though I got the feeling that Tyrell was going to do everything he could to make me suffer right now. He seemed to enjoy it. To get off on hurting the people around him, every way that he could. I didn't know what kind of diagnosis a doctor might have given him, but he was probably some level of sociopath—some level of removed from his emotions to be able to do everything he had done and still want to keep going. To keep hurting. To keep filling the heads of everyone who had the misfortune of running into him with pain and suffering.

The thought of it was enough to make me sick. Sometimes, I had to remind myself that Mia's father had looked at this man and decided that he was good enough for his daughter. It almost seemed impossible, after everything that he had done, that Vincenzo had ever looked at him and seen anything other than the utter monster that he was, but I knew that it would have been hard for him to trust his instincts when there was that much money on the table. Not that I thought it gave him even a hint of an excuse, but at least it made a little more sense, right?

I hated this. I lifted my head as far as I could, and saw that my feet were strapped down to this bed too. I had no idea how they had managed to turn this place into a cell so quickly—or maybe Vincenzo had always used it that way, and I had just decided to overlook it for the time that I had worked with him. I was having to come to terms with the fact that, like it or not, I had chosen to ignore a lot of what my old boss had done with his time because it had just been too horrible to consider.

I was never going to let my guard down like that again. I had learned the hard way that all of this had happened because I had chosen to throw my lot in with someone who had caused more chaos in this city than all of the bad winters combined. It was never going to happen again. As soon as I got out of here—if I was able to get out of here—I was going to fix that, and I was never going to look back again.

The door opened, and I glanced over to see a man that I recognized—Vincenzo's physician. His face was drawn and white and he looked as though he was going to sick. I didn't blame him. He must have been scared shitless right now. I opened my mouth to greet him, but he shook his head sharply, telling me to stay quiet. I closed my eyes, but not entirely—I needed to be aware—once more and sank my head back against the pillow. It was good to see a friendly face, even if it was one as obviously terrified as that.

He was swiftly followed by Tyrell, who was glancing down at his watch and seemed distracted by something. Had he already found a buyer for my time? I had no idea, but if he had, I was well, truly, and totally fucked. I had no idea what to expect, no idea how many favors I might have to call in to get out of there in one piece, but I could do it. I was sure of it. I could make it out of this in one piece, I just had to keep pushing forward. I had to keep making sure that I didn't lose hope. Mia was out there, somewhere, using her wits to stay alive, and she needed me to do the same thing.

"Just patch him up," Tyrell snapped at Ian, the physician, who stepped over to me and peeled back the dressing on the wound of the arm that was throbbing with such pain. He winced when he saw it. Shit, that wasn't good news, surely.

"It's badly infected," he said as Tyrell looked over at him. "I think it would be best to get him to a hospital—"

"We don't have time for that," Tyrell replied. "I'm not asking you to save his life. I just need you to make sure he stays alive for another day, maybe two. Can you do that?"

"I can try—"

"That's all I need to hear," he snapped and went back to looking at his phone like there were far more important things going on in the world right now. He didn't even seem aware that I was awake.

Good! That was how I wanted to keep it. I knew that I had to do everything I could to make sure that I kept myself off his radar. He would try to talk to me, try to get information out of me if he knew that I was alive, and that was the very last thing that I needed right now. I had some idea of where Mia would have gone to, and, though I would never have told him in good faith, I didn't know what tricks he might have had up his sleeve to get me to talk if he could manage it.

The doctor pulled the dressing away from my wound, and I sneaked a look down at it. Fuck, it was a strange color. The infection must have been pretty bad. I had no idea when it had started, but I could already feel the pain throbbing down my arm, right to the tips of my fingers. I had to press my lips together to keep from letting out a groan of pain as the doctor went in to pull out the stitches that were holding my skin together. This hadn't hurt so much when Mia had been the one doing it. Maybe because she had been there, and everything felt as though it was easier to survive if she was right there to keep me company through all of it.

I gritted my teeth as the doctor cleaned out the wound. I knew that I would just have to keep my shit together right now, make sure that Tyrell didn't see any reason to come over and taunt me like I knew that he would want to. Fuck! I hated this guy so much that it made my head hurt. How was I meant to keep my mouth shut when all I wanted to do was fire back at him and tell him that he was a fucking pig? A creep? An animal who would never get Mia to love him no matter how hard he might have tried?

I guessed that he must have caught sight of me glaring at him as the doctor went to work on my arm, because he strode over to the bed and looked down at me with a smile on his face.

"Well, if you aren't back to the land of the living," he remarked. He sounded almost perky. I had no idea how he managed to keep up this facade, this act like he wasn't some sort of monster. Did he really enjoy all of this as much as he made it out? He sure as hell acted like it. I knew that he must have been delighted to have me here. I had no idea who he was going to sell me to, who he was going to pass me along to, but I had plenty of enemies in this town, and I had no doubt that he was going to make the very most of that.

"Good to see you again, Gabe," he remarked, ignoring the wince of pain I let out as the doctor pulled a thread through my arm. "Sorry about your arm, though. Looks like it's going to have to come off. Not that you're going to be alive to see it."

I didn't reply. I didn't want to give him the pleasure of knowing that he was getting under my skin. I closed my eyes and thought of Mia, but even that was enough to make it worse. If I weren't there to protect her, then who would be? The whole world would turn upside down to find her if he implied for an instant that he wanted her back, and she wouldn't be able to hide forever.

"I haven't decided who I'm going to hand you over to yet," he mused out loud, clearly not caring that I wasn't so much as looking at him. "I have a few options, as I'm sure you know. A few people to choose from. Plenty who would do anything for just an hour alone with you, Gabriel. How does that make you feel?"

I didn't reply. My mind was too busy racing, trying to work out who he might have been trying to use against me. I knew that I had enemies in this city, but how many of them would deign to work with a man like Ransom to get their hands on me?

"And how do you think it's going to be for Mia, Gabriel?" he continued, that sick smile spreading even wider across his face.

"Do you think she's going to keep fighting once she sets eyes on your corpse?"

I tried not to let his words get under my skin, but it was too damn hard to ignore them. He knew what he was doing to me. He knew that bringing her up was enough to send sharp stabs of pain through my system. And he knew that I would have done anything … anything at all to make sure that she didn't have to go through what he was threatening me with right now. She deserved better than that. She always had.

And I just had to promise myself that she would battle on, even when she knew what had happened to me. She was stronger than anyone else I had ever met in this business. And she could survive anything that Ransom tried to throw at her.

Chapter Fourteen

Mia

"AND THAT'S THE LAST you saw of him?" Kline asked me, as I finished filling her in what had led me back to her place.

I nodded. "On the balcony, with Ransom," I told her. "He was still alive when I left, but..."

"But with a guy like Tyrell, you don't know how long that's going to last," she finished up for me.

I nodded. "No idea."

"Shit," Kline muttered, as she patted the head of Colonel beside her. Jasmine was hugging her arms around her knees and staring into space on the floor before her, as though she couldn't believe all of this was happening. I reached out to touch her arm, but she jumped, and I realized that she was too scared to be touched in that moment.

"Why did you come here?" she asked me.

I shook my head. "I didn't know where else to go," I admitted. "And this was the only safe place that I could think of. You're the only one in this city who I can trust, Kline. Gabriel made me promise that I wasn't going to give up, no matter what happened to him. I'm not going to let him down."

Kline nodded. She seemed satisfied with that answer. But there was more for us to handle before this conversation was over, and we both knew it.

"What are you going to do to get Gabriel out of there?" she asked me.

I sighed. "I don't know what we can do," I admitted. "I've had ... some thoughts, but they're crazy."

"Crazy is all we've got right now," Kline replied. "Tell me."

"If you can call in any favors that you might be owed," I explained. "We could try and charge the house. Take it over by force. I know that Gabe took out a few of Tyrell's men before I ran, and there will be some out on the roads looking for me now. If we're going to strike, it should be now, while his defenses are down."

Kline leaned back in her seat. She seemed to be calculating the odds of a plan like that. I knew that it was out-there, and that it would probably get most everyone involved injured or worse, but I didn't know what else we could do. And I was sure as hell not going to leave Gabe there to deal with Tyrell alone. Even if he was—even if Ransom had already done his worst—I wanted to see him one more time. I wanted to say my goodbyes.

"I can't do that," Jasmine blurted out. I looked over at her.

"I'm not asking you to," I promised her. "You've already done more than enough for me. You should go, I don't want you getting hurt."

"I can call you a cab," Kline offered her. "You might have to ditch the car here for a while to be on the safe side, but we can get you home, if you need out."

Jasmine looked up at me. Her eyes were glossy with tears. My heart ached for her. She had already been through so much for me. I didn't want her to have to do this too. I didn't want her to feel like she had no choice but to fight for me.

"I don't want that," she replied, firmly, her voice taking on an edge of certainty that made everything feel a little safer. "I want to be here with you. I promised Gabriel that I was going to help you any way that I could. I'm not going to fuck that up."

I closed my eyes and got down on the floor beside her. I didn't know what the hell I had done to deserve a friend like Jasmine, but I was never going to stop being grateful for it. She was everything that I had ever wanted in a best friend, and I was never going to forget how far she had gone for me, how much she had done for me. I loved her, and I was never going to let her forget that.

"Thank you," I murmured, and she nodded. Her jaw was set tight now, as though she had made her mind up and nothing was going to change that.

"What happens now?" she asked and rose to her feet.

"I think you should go and get a shower and some rest," Kline told her firmly. "We might need to pick your brain about the current layout of the house, and I want you to be on fighting form if we do."

"Fighting form?" Jasmine asked, her eyes widening.

"Figure of speech," Kline assured her, standing to her feet. "Here, this way to the bathroom. Clean yourself up. Who knows how long it's going to be before you get a chance to again…"

Jasmine followed her out of the room, and, when Kline returned and sat next to me, she looked more certain than she had before.

"Okay, so, if we're going to get Gabriel out of there, we have to act fast," she explained. "I don't know much about Tyrell, but if I know one thing, it's that he's not going to fuck around and wait any longer than he has to in order to take what he wants."

"Agreed," I replied. "So how quickly can you get your men together?"

"For one, they're not my men," she reminded me. "I don't really have a horse in this race anymore. I used to work with Gabriel back in the day, but that was it. I'm not part of it anymore. I don't know how many of those guys will still remember me, but they might remember Gabriel."

"And you think they would help?" I asked hopefully. I had no idea what to expect with all of this. If she had just laughed in my face and told me that my plan was insane and I needed to give up on it once and for all, I wouldn't have blamed her. But I couldn't give up on him. Not on Gabriel. Not when I knew that he would never have given up on me.

He had come to that house to save me, and now, I was going to do the same to help him.

"Yes, but I'm not sure that you're going to like them much."

"I don't care about that," I replied at once. "Why? It's not like there are many people in this business I care for..."

"They're Donnie's men."

I caught my breath. Of everything that I had expected to come out of her mouth, that was about the last.

"Donnie's men?" I asked, and she nodded.

"They used to work with Gabriel, back in the day," she explained. "They probably still have some love left for him from that. The shit that those guys got involved in, I'd be surprised if they hadn't made a bond for life."

She shook her head and grimaced. One of these days, I was going to have to ask Gabriel just what he had done when he had been working with Donnie. But I could figure that out if I ever got a chance to see him again.

"And now that they're out from under Donnie's thumb, they're going to have more freedom to help him the way they might want to," she explained. "I have no idea if they still hate Gabe as much as Donnie did, but it's the closest thing we've got to a shot right now."

"Then I don't want to blow it," I replied. "How long will it take you to get in touch with them?"

"I'm not sure," Kline replied. "Might be a few hours to get them all together. We might not have everyone on board, some of them are probably working other jobs right now, but if that's the best we can get—"

"Then that's the best we can get," I finished up for her, leaning back in my seat and running a hand through my hair. I didn't know what to expect from these people who had once worked with him. He had told me that he had been a different man back then, but most of these guys had stayed in that business that he had decided to run from. How bad was it? How bad were they?

I tried not to focus on that. All that mattered was that we could pull together some people who would be willing to help us break Gabe out of that place. If he was even still alive—

No, no, no. No thinking like that. Unless I had unequivocal proof that he was dead, I was going to go on the assumption that he was still alive and kicking. Preferably kicking Tyrell right in his fucking head, actually.

Kline must have seen the rush of thoughts inside my head. She reached over and put her hand on my knee.

"We can get him out of there," she promised me. I had no idea if she actually believed it, but that didn't matter right now. I just had to get her on my side long enough to get in touch with those men who she believed would help, and then all of this would be over. I knew that we might have been running out of time, with every second that passed putting Gabe in more danger, but we were going as fast as we could right now.

"I know we can," I replied firmly. "So, what do you need me to do?"

"I need you to hold down the fort here," she replied. "Get your friend to tell us everything that she can about the state of that place when you left it. We're going to need to be able to wrap our heads around it comfortably if we're going to take it the way I want to."

"Perfect," I replied, even though it felt like anything but. "And what are you going to do?"

"I'm going to call in every favor that I have in this town," she explained. "And I'll hit up my brother, too, see if he's got anything that he can give us. It's going to be..."

She trailed off as she rose to her feet. For the first time since I had met her, she actually looked scared. I couldn't say that I blamed her. This was one of the most terrifying things that I had ever done. I had thought that fleeing from my father's place was scary enough, but this was eating that alive in terms of terror.

"I know that we can do this," she told me again. She seemed as much trying to convince herself as she was me, and I nodded again. I needed to believe it the same way she did. I needed to believe that we could do this, because the alternative was too much for me to even handle thinking about.

"Of course we can," I replied firmly. And I wondered how many times the two of us were going to keep saying that to each other until we actually started to believe it. I knew that making it through the next day without losing our minds was going to be near impossible. But if anyone could make this work, it was Kline. I trusted her completely. Almost as much as I trusted Gabriel.

And I knew that we were his last hope of getting out of there in one piece. And there was no way in fucking hell that I was going to pass up the chance to make that happen.

Chapter Fifteen

Gabriel

MY HEAD WAS THROBBING as I came to once again. I could barely remember where the hell I actually was—until I tried to lift my hands to my head to massage my temples, and I realized that they were still shackled below me.

"You need to stay as still as you can," a man ordered me. I looked up and there was Ian, the doctor, still standing beside me. I managed to focus on him. I could feel the heat washing in waves through my system, and I shook my head at him.

"I can't," I replied. It felt as though tiny bugs were sprinting underneath my skin, and I needed to stop them. Were they really there? My head was hurting enough that I could barely process it. I hated this. I was unable to do anything to stop this, unable to do anything to help myself. I strained at the ties once more and gave Ian a hard look.

"You can let me go," I told him.

"You couldn't get far even if I did," he replied apologetically. "You—the fever. It's been spiking all night long. If you were to stand up, you wouldn't make it very far. Your body is trying to heal, but I don't know if it can, not under these conditions."

"Shit, Doc, don't sugarcoat it for me," I remarked, trying to make a joke out of this and failing. He didn't smile. I winced again as the pain jolted up my arm. I couldn't handle this. I knew that everything hinged on how this was going to go, how the next few hours unfolded, but that

Ransom was not, under any circumstances, about to let me get away with what I was doing right now.

"You need to rest," he ordered me. It was strange to think that this man had once worked for Vincenzo. Did he feel guilt, betraying him like this? Or was it just another violent man for him to work for, another way for him to make his wage? I almost wanted to ask him, but my energy was beginning to sap, and I knew that I had to keep it fighting fit for when I got a chance to see Mia again.

Mia. At least I had that to fall back on. She would have been far from here now, and that was all that I cared about. I prayed that Tyrell hadn't managed to get his hands on her and Jasmine, and I was so thankful that she had a best friend as brave as she was to stand by her side. The two of them could be halfway across the state by now, or the country, I didn't really know how long I had been out for. I just needed to believe that she was safe. I just needed to keep that at the front of my mind, no matter what.

"Did he say anything to you?" I asked Ian. "About what he's going to do to me?"

Ian slid his eyes away from me. He didn't have to tell me. He knew that it was going to be bad, and that was all that he could say about it. I wondered how many people had battled for the price on my head, for the revenge that they thought that they were owed against me. I hated this. I wanted to tear the restraints loose, but they were bound too tightly, and my body was starting to give out from beneath me. Betraying me, after all this time, after everything I had put it through—when I needed it the most, it was letting me down, and I hated it more than anything.

Suddenly, I heard the door open behind Ian. Whoever it was reached inside and flicked off the light switch. Tyrell had always been one for the amateur fucking dramatics, but this was a little overboard, even for him.

"Doc. Out."

Ian lingered for another moment. He might have worked in a shady-ass industry, but he was still a doctor, and it was clear that he didn't want to leave me, a patient of his, without treatment. Tyrell raised his voice and repeated what he had to say, and this time, the doctor backed out of the room, and left me alone with the man who wished me nothing but harm.

"How are you feeling, Gabriel?" Tyrell asked me, as the door closed behind him. I tried to peer up at him in the darkness, but it was too black in there to make out where he was even standing. He probably wanted me spooked, feeling lost and out of control. I hated him. But I was sure that he wasn't the only person in the room with us right now.

"Fine," I spat back at him, even though it was a lie. I didn't want to give him the satisfaction of knowing the pain that I was in right now. Knowing this fucking creep, he would probably get off on it, being certain of how badly I was suffering.

Beside him, a light—just for a moment, someone puffing on a cigar. It was something expensive. Even in the mess that my senses were in, I could tell that. But I couldn't make out who was standing beside him. Though, surely, this would be the man who had paid to make sure that he got his hands on me before anyone else.

"I'm glad to hear it," Tyrell replied brightly. He sounded almost giddy with excitement. Like he could hardly wait to share his news with me.

"I have someone who wants to meet with you, Gabriel," he explained, and he flicked on the light. And it was at that moment that I saw who was right there beside him. And, as soon as I did, I felt my stomach drop.

"What the fuck," I muttered, mostly to myself. It took me a moment to place the rotund older man in front of me, puffing on a cigar, but when I saw the hatred in his eyes, I knew that he could only be one person.

"You must remember Sal, right?" Tyrell asked, gesturing to his companion. "As in, Sal, father of Damien?"

"The man you murdered?" Sal spat at me, as he blew out a plume of smoke in my direction. His face was twisted into a mask of sheer fury, and the sight of him like that was enough to send a shiver down my spine. If there was anyone who had a score to settle with me, it was him.

"I didn't kill your son," I reminded him, trying to think as fast as my addled brain would allow. "Vincenzo ordered the hit—"

"And you're the one who carried it out," he replied. "Because you say that he put hands on that slut of a daughter of his. She probably wanted it, but you couldn't handle the thought of her desiring someone else, could you? So you killed him."

My vision blurred with fury. I wasn't sure if it was the way he was talking about Mia, or something else, but I wanted to get to my feet and land a punch on his face. He just couldn't handle the thought that he had raised a kid who would do something as foul as what Damien had done to Mia. If anyone had deserved to die, out of all the people who I had killed, that man was one of them. And I would never apologize for it. I had probably saved dozens of women from his slippery hands—or worse.

"How much to kill him?" Sal asked Tyrell bluntly.

Tyrell shook his head. "I'm not sure that you could afford it, Sal," he replied. He was enjoying this. He was enjoying every second of this. Exploiting a grieving father's pain, selling off my life to him because he knew that he would make a profit. And he was sure that Sal would make me suffer the way he thought I deserved. If there was anyone on earth more foul than Ransom Tyrell, I had yet to meet them. But when I did, I would make sure that they knew what a piece of shit they were to me.

"How much?" Sal repeated, slower this time, his voice etched with irritation that Tyrell had dared to question him.

"Hmm," Tyrell remarked, tapping his fingers on his chin, tipping his head back for a moment as he considered the offer. "I suppose we could discuss the cost. Depends how much you're willing to pay."

"To get my hands on him?" Sal shot back. "Anything."

"That's a good place to start," Tyrell agreed. "Though you'd be cheating a lot of people out of revenge, Sal, I'm sure you know that—"

"It's what he deserves." He snarled, and the way he was looking at me, I knew that he would have ripped my head off with his bare hands if he thought that it meant he could be sure that I would never get out of there alive. He might have been a boss, the kind of guy who didn't get his hands dirty any longer, but when it came to his son, I knew that all of that would go out of the window. I had pushed a button that could never be unpushed, and I only had myself to blame for that. I only had myself to blame for following the orders that Vincenzo had given me because I had believed that I was worth nothing more than that.

"Your son got what he deserved," I fired back at him. If I was going to die for Damien, then I was going to make sure that his father knew just what kind of son he had raised.

"Shut your mouth—"

"He begged for his life," I continued. In truth, I could hardly remember what I had done to him, but his father needed to hear it.

"He pleaded with me to let him live," I went on. "He was pathetic. A waste of space. You should be grateful that I took him off your hands."

"You shut your fucking mouth or I'll do it for you, you bastard," Sal exclaimed, and he lunged toward me, but before he could lay a hand on me, Tyrell grabbed his shoulder to hold him back. Clearly not wanting him to injure his prime prize before he'd had a chance to sell it.

"Come on, Sal, let's get a drink and talk about the price," he told him, but Sal was still glaring at me. My vision was starting to get hazy again, but I did my best to meet his gaze. To let him know that he wasn't going to be able to get me to apologize. I had done the world a favor taking out that piece-of-shit son of his, and nothing was going to change my mind on that. He had hurt Mia. And, as far as I was concerned, that was reason enough for him to pay for every mistake he had ever made in his life.

As the two men stalked out of the room once more, I let my head fall back and closed my eyes again. Mia. She was the one who I had to keep at the front of my mind. She was the one I had to do all this for. All the pain, all the suffering, all of it—had happened because of her, and nothing was going to change that.

And nothing was going to change my sureness that I had made the right choice in doing everything that I had done, everything that had brought me to this moment. I might have been scared right now—I might have been sure that I was never actually going to find a way to walk out of that room in one piece again—but she was far from here, and she would be safe by now. And as long as I kept focused on that, nothing else in the world actually mattered to me one little bit.

Chapter Sixteen

Mia

JASMINE HOVERED BY the side of the car. I knew that she wanted to tell me to stop what I was doing, but there was no way in hell I could do that now, not when it finally felt like we were getting somewhere.

"Are you sure you're going to be okay?" Jasmine asked the two of us, and Kline shook her head cheerfully.

"Not at all," she replied. She had been talking like this since the moment that we had left the house to get into the car, and I knew that it wasn't doing anything to soothe Jasmine's nerves.

"We'll be fine," I tried to calm Jasmine, and my best friend leaned in the window of the car and eyed me for a moment.

"And if you're not?"

"You need to go," I told her as gently as I could. I knew that she wasn't going to listen to a word that came out of my mouth, but I didn't care. I needed to make sure that she was as far from this place as she could possibly be. I knew that she was scared, and I didn't want even a second of her pain on my conscience.

"Please just stay safe, okay?" she fussed over me, and she leaned farther in through the window and gave me a hug.

"I'll do everything I can," I promised her. "Really. Now, get out of here. I don't want anyone to find you here if they come looking."

She nodded, smoothed her hair back, and headed over to the small blue coupe that she had driven me here in. Not much of a getaway car, but hopefully it's low-key nature would mean that she could make an easy escape in it.

"Good friend you've got there," Kline remarked, as I rolled up the window.

I nodded. "I know," I replied. "I don't know what I'd have done without her."

"All the more reason to make sure that you get out of this un-scathed," she replied, and she pulled out of the driveway and down the street.

It was four in the morning, and a few houses were glowing with light, but most were still cast into darkness. The city wasn't awake yet, and I had to hope that it went for Tyrell and his men too. Kline and I had spent the last five hours rallying up as many people as we could, as many who would be willing to come fight for Gabriel's freedom with us, and I was pretty sure that we were going to have a miniature army at our disposal when the time came. Which was exactly what I need-ed right now. I knew that it was a long shot, heading down there af-ter they'd already had Gabe for so long, but I wasn't going to let any-thing slip through my fingers. I had been through too much to let this go now.

As Kline and I pulled away from her house, she glanced at me in the mirror.

"You don't have to do this, you know," she told me quietly.

I shook my head. "I don't have a choice."

"You do," she reminded me. "And I think I'd be a bad friend to Gabriel if I didn't point out that he'd tell you to turn around and get out of this city while you still can."

"I'd be a worse one if I took that advice," I replied. Though I knew Gabe and I were far more than friends now. I didn't want to even con-sider the possibility of what might have come next. Just like I didn't want to consider the possibility of how dark my life would have gotten if I found out that I could have done something to save him, and hadn't.

I would never be able to forgive myself. I would never be able to forgive Kline for not letting me go back.

"I suppose so," she replied with a sigh, and she chuckled and shook her head.

"What are you laughing at?" I asked. Didn't seem much, to me, that was funny about this situation.

"Just that you're as stubborn as him," she pointed out. "I see why the two of you get on so well. Neither of you know what's best for you."

"Or maybe we just know it's each other," I pointed out.

"Maybe," she agreed. I wondered if Kline had ever loved anyone that much. She must have sincerely cared about Gabriel if she was willing to go to the mat for him like this—maybe not in the same way that I did, but that had to count for something. I leaned my head against the window and watched as the sun begin to rise slowly in the distance. It would almost have been peaceful, if it wasn't for how frightened and tense I was in that instant.

I couldn't stop wondering what Gabe was doing. What he might have been enduring. Because whatever it was, there was no way that it was fair. I wished that I could just reach out to him and tell him that we were coming. That he just had to wait a little while longer, and we would be there.

I still didn't know much about the men who had decided to come through for Gabriel this morning, but I knew that I might very well owe them the life of the man I loved. Kline had told me that they had worked for Donnie back in the day alongside Gabriel, back when he had been wrapped up in some seriously dark shit, and they had his back now that he was in danger. Even though a few of them had been deployed against him when Donnie had tried to launch his attack against his old partner.

"Seems like they were only working with Donnie for as long as it took for the old fucker to get put out of the picture permanently," Kline explained to me. I wondered just what she had been through with Donnie to loathe him so much, but those stories could wait. Right now, what mattered was getting to the rendezvous point where we were meeting with the rest of the small army that Kline had managed to pull together for us.

Most of it, she told me, revolved around her brother. It was through him that she had met Gabriel in the first place, and the two of them had become close. Her brother was part of a biker gang who worked alongside Donnie, and he had a whole lot of sway on his side of Chicago, much to my relief. I was just glad that there was someone here who seemed to know what the hell they were doing, because I was groping around in the dark, and Kline had been out of the game for so long she seemed unsure if she could pull it off.

We came to a halt in the parking lot of a non-descript-looking bar—or it would have been nondescript, if it hadn't been for the dozen or so bikers waiting for us. Most were dressed in leathers, a few with obvious weapons bulging in their clothes, and I tried to remind myself that these were the good guys who we needed so badly. No matter how scary they might have seemed to be in that instant.

"Okay, you ready for this?" Kline asked me, and I nodded. I could see a few of them staring at me already, and I wondered if they knew who I was.

Kline strode up toward the man who I assumed was her brother—same red hair, though not quite as bright as hers—and he greeted her with a nod. He didn't look certain about her presence here, and, as his eyes slid over to mine, I figured that he wasn't about mine either.

"I don't ask for much from you," Kline told him, "but I really need your help right now."

"This is about Gabe," I told them, and they seemed to bristle, as though wondering what I was doing with his name in my mouth. They had good reason to wonder. After all, it wasn't exactly as though I looked like the kind of girl who would know Gabriel Hallow, no matter how far in love with him I might have been. If I'd had the time to sit them down and fill them in on the whole story, I would have done that, but I knew that time was of the essence and that we needed to move sooner rather than later.

"You all know Gabriel Hallow, don't you?" Kline announced, looking back and forth between the motley crew in front of her. "Saved a few of your asses a few times, I'd say. So I think you owe him a favor. Or, at least, if you're here, you owe either my brother or me a favor, and this is what we're asking from you."

She took a deep breath, then continued. I noticed that her voice was shaking slightly, as though she could hardly believe that she was having to do this.

"Gabriel is in danger right now," she explained. "He's being held by Ransom Tyrell at what used to be the Romano family mansion. We don't know if he's dead or alive right now, but either way, we're sure as hell not leaving him there to rot."

There was a mumble of surprise around the group. Tyrell was clearly a name that had some reach, even to a place like this. It must have spooked them to hear her talking like that.

"And, much as I'd like to, we can't do that alone," she went on. "So we're going to need your help. It's not going to be easy, and I'm not going to stand here and say that most of you will get out alive, because you all know as well as I do that the chances of that are slim at best."

There was a silence. In the cold of the morning air, I shivered, wrapping my arms around myself. I wished that they were Gabriel's. Well, soon, with any luck, they would be.

"So, how many of you are with us?" Kline asked as she scanned her eyes across the group in front of her. There was a split second of silence, and I thought for one horrible second that none of them were going to step forward and take us on. A few of them had already agreed, but that had been before they knew the parameters of the operation that we were throwing out there, and I wouldn't have been surprised if they had decided that they would really rather fucking not when they discovered the truth.

But then her brother stepped forward. And he nodded. "I'm in," he replied. "And the rest of my men will be too. How long do we have to pull this together?"

"The less time, the better," Kline replied. "We're going down there to scope the place out as soon as this is over, and we want to get in there by midday today. How long is it going to take you to get them in place?"

"We can move in as fast as we can," he replied, and there was a shuffle of agreement in the men around him. Which meant...

"So you'll do it?" she asked, and he nodded.

"What does that mean?" I asked Kline, lowering my voice.

She turned to me, this slightly manic smile on her face, somewhere between fear and excitement.

"That means, my dear Mia," she told me, slapping me on the shoulder. "That you and I are about to go to war."

And whether it was a war that we would win, well, we had yet to see that. But I was going to do everything I could to get the man I loved out of there in one piece. No matter what it took from me.

Even if it took my life.

Chapter Seventeen

Gabriel

"NOW, SAL, YOU DON'T want to spoil all the fun so soon, do you?"

Tyrell's voice cut through the fog of red pain and panic in my head, just before Sal landed another punch on my jaw. My head was lolling down to my chest and I managed to look up for a moment, just long enough that I could connect eyes with the older man. I spat a mouthful of blood out at his feet, and wondered if I would have any teeth left after the beating that he had given me.

"Wouldn't mind it." Sal growled, and he started pulling his arm back to land another strike, but before he could, Tyrell put a hand on his shoulder.

"You've paid for this," he replied. "You deserve to make the most of it that you can. Come on, let's get a drink, something to eat. You can come in with renewed fervor when you're all done."

"Fine," Sal replied, shaking out his hand, which spattered a few drops of blood to the ground as he went. He didn't sound particularly happy about the new state of affairs. I didn't care. It would give me a moment's reprise. Though if that was honestly a better thing or not, I hadn't decided yet. Because I knew that he was going to kill me with his bare hands as soon as he got the chance, and I wasn't sure how much more of this outright torture I could take without caving and begging him to stop.

The two men headed out of the room, shutting the door behind them. I groaned and closed my eyes, but even that was too painful. My skin felt like it were on fire, the pain from the infection growing sharper with every passing second. My blood was pumping in my ears, and I could taste that metallic sensation in my mouth again, where he had burst my lip a few hours before. Or was it a few minutes? I couldn't remember. All I knew was that they had come back here and seemed to have agreed on a price, because Sal had started whaling on me like I was the cause of all of his problems.

Which, I supposed, to him, I likely was. After all, I had killed his son. Even if I knew that it had been Vincenzo, I was the one who had pulled the trigger, and the chances of him getting his hands on the patriarch of the Romano family was slim to none, even in Vincenzo's exposed state. Perhaps he already knew, too, that he had lost his son, and felt as though he had suffered enough.

But that my suffering should only just have been beginning.

How long were they going to keep me like this? I didn't know how much more my body could take. I can put it through the wringer these last few days, and there was only so much I could expect it to do before it gave out entirely. It didn't deserve everything that had happened.

And for what? What had I done this all for? For her. I knew that it had been worth it every time her face crossed my mind once again. It might have been hard, might have been downright terrifying sometimes, might have been almost certain to end my life, but it had been *worth* it. I knew that I would have gone through all of it again and again and once more after that if I could be sure that she was far from Chicago, far from everything that her father had tried to do to her.

He would never get close to her again. That, I was sure of. She was her own woman now, no matter what happened next. She had fought for that right, for everything that she had become, and I knew that nothing was going to change that. Even if Ransom got his hands on her, he would never, ever be able to take that from her. She was better than he would ever be. Better than he ever deserved. And I was proud to have been a part of that, even if I wasn't sure that I would get to see it through the way that I might have wanted to.

If this was the end, then I had gone out on a high. And, as I let the pain wash through me, I felt it begin to recede a little. Maybe this was going to be over sooner than I thought. Maybe this was the end. And if it was...

"Gabe!"

I heard a voice call my name, and I looked up. I half expected it to be Mia, even though I knew that was ridiculous. But instead, as the film in front of my eyes began to clear and I focused once more, I couldn't believe who I saw standing in front of me.

"Ian? Jerry?" I demanded.

"Keep your voice down!" Ian ordered me at once, glancing around like he expected someone to come pouncing out at him at any moment.

"What are you doing here?" I asked, my voice groggy and slurry around the edges.

"We're getting you out."

"You're what?"

"Stop asking questions," Jerry ordered, as he began to untie me from the chair. "We don't have much time. Shit, how many times did they loop this knot?"

"You need to stop," I told them. "You need to—if they catch you here—"

"Then all three of us are as good as dead," Ian finished up for me, as he paced back and forth and kept an eye on the door. "I know that. We both know that. But we can't just let this happen, Gabriel. We need to get you out."

I fell silent. I knew that there was going to be no arguing with them. And besides, why the hell would I argue? If they really wanted to help me, then I wasn't going to stop them. Not a chance in hell. I was going to take every shot that I had to get out of there before they came back.

"We have a few people on the doors to let us know when they're finished their food," Ian explained, almost more to himself than to me. "But we don't have a lot of time before they figure out that we're here."

"You guys have families—"

"And I don't want them to think that I would put up with letting a man like Sal beat you to death when there was something I could have done to help," Jerry replied, and he finally figured out the knot and unwrapped it for good. "Fuck! Finally!"

I rose to my feet, dizzy, my vision blurring and smudging in front of me. Jerry grabbed one of my arms and draped it over his shoulder, guiding me toward the door. My legs were struggling to find purchase on the ground below me. But I was up. And, as Ian took my other arm and started to lead me out of the door, I wondered if this was just some fantasy that my addled brain was feeding me to convince me that it couldn't be as bad as I thought it was. That I could really get out of there.

But if my brain was trying to do me a favor, then there was no way that it would force me to feel the grinding agony that was driving through every corner of my being right now. No, that was real, and that meant the rest of this was too.

Which meant that I was going to get out.

I was too exhausted to be scared, which was probably a good thing. I could feel blood leaking from more parts of me than I could count, and I did my best to ignore them. I could deal with them later. Ian was a doctor, he could help me—if we got out of here in one piece, that was.

I could see a few familiar places out of the corners of my eyes. Okay, I knew that one, that one, that one. I was getting closer to the back entrance, I was sure of it. It wouldn't be long till I was in the garden, and hopefully they had thought far enough ahead to get some people out there to take me away. I needed to get as far from this place as I possibly could before Ransom and Sal worked out that I was gone, and I didn't much feel like risking being dragged back to an even worse fate if they discovered that I had made a break for it.

Mia. I would get to see Mia gain. The thought pierced through everything else in my brain, clear as day, and a smile spread across my face. A big, stupid, sloppy smile, the kind that only came when everything else was wiped away by the feeling of joy inside me right now. I couldn't believe it. I had been so sure that all of this was over for us. That the best I could hope for as far as Mia was concerned was the sureness that she had gotten out alive. But I might get to be with her again. I had no idea what that would look like, how long it would take, if she even knew that I was alive right now, but for the time being, just focusing on that thought was all that mattered to me.

My feet were hardly touching the ground as Ian and Jerry continued to drag me through the house. I wondered who else they had managed to get on their side with all of this. I would have to find out as soon as I got the chance, and make sure that they knew I owed them my life and would never forget it. Not that I believed that any single one of them would want to see me again after this. Not after I had caused so much trouble for them.

We reached the back door at last, and Ian had just put his hand on the handle when a noise cut through the quiet.

Gunfire. Ian jumped so hard he nearly dropped me, and Jerry cursed under his breath. My stomach plummeted. Just how close was that to us? Ransom's voice soon followed, furious, full of rage, screaming into the silence that came as they reloaded their weapons.

"Get out there and stop them!" he demanded. But I was sure that he wasn't talking about us. That gunfire had come from the front of the house,

"Did you give anyone a gun?" I asked Jerry, and he shook his head.

"No," he replied. "That's nothing to do with us."

"But who..." I murmured, and then it hit me. Who the hell would want to come to this place and try to take it? The man who owned it, of course. Vincenzo Romano. I had asked him to hold off a little while longer while I got Mia out of there, but he had clearly run out of patience and was ready to take back what was his.

But that might just give us the cover we needed to get the hell out of there. And I would take anything that I was given right now.

"Keep going!" Jerry hissed. "Out the back, come on, we can't stop now!"

"You're right," Ian muttered, and he opened the door and dragged me out behind him. I tried to stay on my feet as the sun hit me full force. But I didn't care. It couldn't stop the smile on my face. Because I was sure that I was going to get a chance to see Mia again. And I couldn't think of anything much better in the world right now than that.

Chapter Eighteen

Mia

"SHIT!" I EXCLAIMED, jumping in my seat as I heard another flurry of bullets from toward the house. "What the hell is that?"

"We're about to find out," Kline replied grimly as she ducked her head to peer under the glare of the sun and see what the hell was going on up at the house.

It was the second round of gunfire that we'd heard since we'd turned onto the street to take the mansion back. I had no idea if some of our guys had managed to go up ahead, but they wouldn't have started the attack without us. No, whatever was happening, it had nothing to do with us. And I didn't like that one little bit.

"We need to go," Kline ordered me, and she put her foot on the pedal and pulled open the glove box to grab the gun that she had stashed there. She pushed it into my hand.

"You need to get ready," she warned me. "You think you can handle this?"

"Shouldn't we wait and see what's going on there first?" I asked.

She shook her head. "We don't have time for that."

I closed my hand around the cool metal of the gun, and, to my surprise, I actually felt a wash of calm spread through my body. Okay. I could do this. Whatever happened, happened. It was going to end here and now, once and for all. After everything that had happened, everything that we had all been through, it was going to end right back where it started. At this house. Where I had always belonged.

Kline led the stream of bikers behind us up to the house, and I lifted a hand to stop her when I saw the car that was sitting outside. I recognized it. It was the same brand that my father always got his drivers to use. Which meant that...

"I think it's my father!" I exclaimed. "Trying to take the house back."

"Fuck," she muttered. "He's not going to be pleased to see us."

"We're here for different things, but we can help each other," I pointed out quickly, as I pushed the gun into the band of my pants. "Let me talk to him. Once he works out what we're doing, he's not going to try and stop us."

I climbed out before Kline could stop me, and I hurried toward the car that I was sure my father was in, keeping my head down and trying to ignore the stream of gunfire that was coming from the front of the house. I could hear Tyrell barking commands, and I grinned at the fear in his voice. Good. He should be scared. Because the whole might of what remained of the Romano family was going to come right down on his head.

I banged on the car door, and, sure enough, a moment later, it sprang open—and I found myself face to face with my father. I had thought, for a while, that I might never get to see him again, and some part of me wanted to throw my arms around him and tell him that I was glad that he was alive. But we had bigger and better things to think about right now, and I wasn't going to let anything get in the way of that.

"Mia, what the hell are you doing here?" he demanded. I could see the confusion in his eyes, too, trying to make that choice between hugging me and telling me to get the fuck out of there.

"I'm here to get Gabriel," I told him swiftly. "I have men with me."

"What men—"

"Just trust me on this," I replied. "They're bikers. All I'm asking is that you don't get in the way of what we're trying to do. Can you manage that?"

He nodded. He knew that we didn't have time to waste and he wasn't going to let this slip through my fingers.

"How long has he had Gabriel for?" he asked.

I shook my head. "I don't know exactly," I replied.

"He's not going to be—"

"I don't care what kind of state he's in," I told him firmly. "I just want to get him out. Can you work with me on this?"

"I can work with you," he replied. He knew as well as I did that we didn't have time for any big arguments. We just had to find a way to make this work without getting in each other's way. We would serve as distractions to each other's missions, and right now, that was the best that I could ask for.

"Great," I replied. "Tell your men not to come after mine, and I'll tell mine not to go after yours."

"Okay."

"And Dad?"

"What is it?" he asked me.

I narrowed my eyes at him. "I'm the one giving the orders now," I told him. "You understand me? Don't try and get in my way."

"I won't," he agreed at once.

I grinned. I couldn't imagine him giving me that space before. Up until that moment, I had still just been his daughter, unable to take care of anything without his help or that of my brother. But now, I was here to fight. And I wasn't going to let anyone get in the way of that.

"Thank you," I replied. I paused for a moment to look over the mess that was happening in the garden in front of us. I could make out a few figures that I recognized. Over by the house, there were a stack of security men who I remembered from the party a few months ago where Damien had groped me. Maybe his family was working with Tyrell or something? I had no idea. I just needed to get back to Kline and tell her that we had my father and his troops on our side, even if it might have been an uneasy alliance right now.

I'm coming, Gabe. I'm coming.

I wished that I could tell where he was. It would have made everything easier if I could just close that gap between us and get to him sooner rather than later. But if I had to turn that whole house upside down to make sure of it, then I would. I didn't care what it took. I grabbed the gun from my waistband, and something caught my eye.

I looked over into the garden and spotted a figure—a familiar one. For a split second, I thought that it might have been Gabe, but when I looked over to follow it, I couldn't help but smile. It was Glo. She was stalking through the garden like a lioness, gun in hand, ready to take out anyone who got in her way. And I knew that my father really meant business if he had pulled her into this. She was the last person I would have wanted to come up against in a fight like this one. She moved with total confidence, like she already knew that she owned the place. Occasionally she gestured to the men around her, as if to tell them to move a little closer to the house so she could get a better shot off at the people who were protecting the mansion.

I slid back into the car next to Kline, out of breath.

"He said that he'd work with us," I told her quickly. "As long as we don't get in his way."

"I'll tell them," Kline replied, and she rolled out of the car, gun in hand, keeping herself low. I heard her talking to her brother, and I felt my heart pounding in my chest. And it wasn't just because I knew that I was so close to getting to Gabe once more. But it was that I was able to put together something like this. A few months ago, I would have been scared to go out of my front door without my father's permission. But these days, I didn't have to ask for it. I knew that I was in control. I knew that I ran this shit.

I had to focus on how to get through this right now. I had no idea what the next step was. We had a better chance of making it now that my father was in on this, too, but I still didn't totally believe that we could make this happen. There was a big block in my mind between this moment right here and the one where I had my arms around Gabriel. I knew that I would likely have to kill to get there, but I would do it if I had to. In fact, if I got to look down the barrel to Tyrell's face and make him pay for everything he had done to me, to my family, to the man that I loved so much, then I wouldn't wait another second to take what I needed from him.

Kline emerged next to the car once more and gave me a sharp nod.

"We're ready when you are."

"Good," I replied. "Let's do this."

Kline jerked her head toward the group behind her, and a moment later, a small army of bikers swarmed past the car and toward the house. I leaped out to join them, hot on their heels, my feet bouncing off the asphalt as though I was made of air. My hands were clamped around the gun and my mouth was set into a hard line and I promised myself that I was going to do whatever it took. Whatever it took to get Gabriel out of there in one piece.

We burst through the front gate, and, in a flurry of gunfire, we made it up the driveway toward the house. The place was already decimated. The car Gabriel had driven was still sticking out the front of the house, as well as shattered glass from gunshots that had penetrated the windows. I felt nothing at the sight of the home that I used to call my own being torn to pieces. I had no connection to it any longer, because I had no connection to the woman that I had been when I lived here. No, not the woman, the girl—the child, basically. Because I had only become the adult that I was right now when I had broken free of this place. When I had promised myself that I would never come slinking back here. Not for my father, not for Ransom, not anyone.

Kline led me into the house, and she and the bikers cleared out a handful of Ransom's guards who were still trying to hold down the fort. The man himself was nowhere to be seen, and I wouldn't have been surprised if that fucking coward had fled and left his men to pick up the pieces. He might have talked a big game, but when it came down to it, I knew that he wouldn't dare stand up to all of this. The Romano family was here to fuck his shit up, and that was the end of it. We weren't going to let him get away with everything he had done to us. To Vinnie. To Gabe. To me.

I looked around. I needed to find Gabe. Where the hell was he? Still upstairs? I knew that I couldn't go up there alone, and my head was throbbing with the sound of gunfire, so I knew that even if I called his name, I wouldn't have been able to hear him right now.

I paused for a moment, gathered myself, and closed my eyes. I was so close to him. I could feel it. I just needed to push a little further, a little longer. And I would have him in my arms again soon.

Chapter Nineteen

Gabriel

"SHIT!" JERRY HISSED, as he heard the explosion of gunfire around the front of the building. Voices were closing in around the backyard, and I knew that we were going to have to get back inside the house if we were going to make it out of there in one piece.

"Go to the study!" I ordered them both, wincing as I tried to turn myself around to get out of there. The two of them did as they were told, grabbing me by the arms and leading me in the direction of Vincenzo's study. It was the best bet for us right now, the safest place in this whole building. He had built it to make sure that it would withstand anything in the way of attacks from his enemies. But hopefully, it would stand up to an assault by him too.

I tried to focus on how to get out of there, but the pain that was rushing through my system was impossible to deny. My head was still spinning and I felt weak and woozy, a sure sign that I was losing a lot of blood and probably didn't have long left.

"We need to hide," Jerry told Ian, once they had managed to push me into the study.

"We need to get him to a hospital," Ian shot back angrily, as though irritated that he even had to argue this point any longer.

"If we go out there now, all of us are going to get killed," I warned him bluntly. "The best thing we can do is buckle down for as long as we can and wait for this to cool off."

"You need to get proper treatment," Ian replied, but he must have known that arguing wasn't going to get him far.

"I've made it this long," I pointed out. "What's another fifteen minutes?"

"It could be the difference as to whether you live or die," he replied sharply. I ignored him. It wasn't as though I had much of a choice right now.

"Barricade the doors," I ordered Jerry, and I sank back against the desk to catch my breath. I felt like every single step I took was another that stripped something out of me, wrung me a little drier, but what else could I do? I had no choice but to push, to keep pushing, to hope for the best and pray that this, somehow, turned out the way I needed it to.

Mia. She was everything I had to stay focused on right now. I didn't care what it took, I was going to get a chance to see her again. No matter what it stripped out of me, no matter how long I had to fight, no matter how hard it was. I could sense her, how near she was, and I wasn't going to let her slip through my fingers now. Not when I had come so close to getting everything that I needed from her.

I knew that there were weapons in the office, and I intended to make the very most of them that I could. We just had to act fast and make sure we were armed against whoever tried to come through that door. I had no idea exactly who was in the house, whether they would have been sympathetic to our plight or if they would have torn us a new one if they found us there. I just had to hope that it was the former. Though I had never much liked to rely on hope to get me out of a bad situation.

I tried to still my breathing, but it was getting harder and harder to control it as the pain began to arch through me again. I needed pain relief, I was sure of it. Ian was right, if I didn't get treatment soon, I might not be able to walk out of this place at all. The clouds were starting to form at the corners of my eyes, and I knew that it was a sure sign that things were beginning to slip away from me. But what else could I do?

I didn't have a choice right now. If I stepped out of there, if I moved to escape, there would be a dozen people ready and waiting to gun me down the first chance that they got.

Even if it was Vincenzo. I knew that he still must have held such anger at me for everything that had happened between us, even if I weren't the one who had stolen Mia this time around, I was the one who had stolen her before, and it would take a long time before he forgave me. I didn't blame him. I had betrayed him in the worst way that I possibly could have. And I just had to pray now that, against all the odds, he saw fit to forgive me even after the mess that I had made of his daughter's life.

There was a crash against the door, which Jerry had just managed to brace with one of the chairs. It shuddered dangerously as it tried to hold the door shut, and Ian jumped.

"What are we going to do?" He hissed. I gestured for him to keep his voice down, and keyed in the code to one of the drawers that held the guns that Vincenzo kept in here. I pulled two out, handed one to Jerry, and checked that the other was loaded. I lifted my finger to my lips. If we could keep quiet enough, then there was a chance that they would just lose interest and move on.

But then, all at once, another strike landed on the door. This time sharper than before, louder. Ian jumped again. I could tell that he was starting to regret getting involved in this little escape attempt. I didn't blame him. He had signed up to get me out of there, not to see off an army currently trying to break down the door.

"It's going to be okay," I assured him as best as I could, but I knew that I couldn't say that and mean it. Ian had a family, so did Jerry. I wasn't going to let both of them sacrifice their safety just to be here with me.

"You need to get out," I told Ian, and then I looked over at Jerry. "Both of you. You need to get as far from here as you possibly can."

"No, we don't," Jerry replied grimly, but Ian looked as though he might have had something else to say about that.

"I'm not letting you stay here and get hurt by all of this," I warned them both. "I'm not having that on my conscience."

"How the hell are we meant to get out?" Jerry hissed at me, nodding toward the door. "I don't think that they're just going to let us walk past them..."

"The window," I replied, and I moved to the other side of the room, where a small window looked out on to the yard beyond. I peered out, and much to my relief, it didn't seem as though the troops who had arrived here had made it that far yet.

"If you go now, you'll be able to make it out the back before anyone notices you," I promised them both. "But you have to move now. Come on..."

"I'm not leaving you to deal with all of this alone," Jerry told me firmly, and I shook my head.

"And I'm not telling your family that you died trying to protect someone like me," I replied. He paused for a moment. Though I was sure he had plenty more he would have liked to say to me right then, he seemed to accept that I had a point. His family cared about him, and I didn't want to have to be the one to deliver the news that he had taken a bullet trying to keep someone like me from the chop.

"This way," I ordered them, and I managed to inch the window just far enough open that we could pry it away from the frame and push it to the ground outside—there were another few bangs at the door as the people trying to catch us in the act attempted to break in, but I ignored them. All that mattered was getting the two of them out in one piece. I wasn't going to risk being the reason that either of them got hurt.

"You get to a hospital as soon as you can, all right?" Jerry ordered me, and I nodded.

"I will," I promised. I didn't know if I would last that long, but I knew that he needed to hear it from me right now.

"Thanks for your help," I told them both. It seemed a weak-ass comment given how much they had done for me, how much they had put on the line to help me, but I couldn't think of anything else to say in that moment.

"You can buy us both a drink when you're out the other side, okay?" Jerry told me, and he squeezed my shoulder, furrowing his brow as he looked into my eyes.

"Okay," I promised them, and I nodded to the window. "Now—out of here. Get as far as you can, as fast as you can. I don't need to worry about the two of you as well."

I watched as Ian scrambled out first, almost going face-first into the gravel outside as he tried to find his feet, and Jerry was quick to follow him, making it out a few seconds later. He turned to face me as he tucked the gun into the waistband of his pants and gave me a sharp nod.

"Get out of there," he ordered me, and I knew that he wasn't going to take anything else for an answer. I nodded right back at him.

"I will," I replied, and with that, the two of them finally turned to make a break for it across the yard. I could hear gunfire from around the front of the house, but hopefully, it would be trapped there for a little while, a small war of attrition as everyone tried to get their asses out of there in one piece. Which I knew is all that they would care about for the time being—for as much as everyone would have liked to pretend that they were loyal and that they would have done anything to assure that their bosses came out on top, when the bullets were flying, there was only one thing that mattered, and that was getting yourself out alive.

Which was what I had to stay focused on right now too. I had to get out of there in one piece. I had to find Mia. I didn't know where she might have been right now, or if she was in danger or not, but I needed to find her, and I was going to do anything and everything that it took to ensure that I got her again. That I got back to her the way that I knew we both deserved.

There was another crack at the door, and the chair buckled dangerously. I checked that my gun was loaded one more time, and inhaled a long, deep breath. I could do this. No matter what it took, I could do this. I could do anything if it meant that I got out of there alive.

I let out the breath that I had been holding and swore to myself that this was far from over yet. As far from over as it could possibly be. Even though I felt like I was going to give out on the spot, I could do this. I could make this. I could survive it.

If I got her at the other side of it all.

Chapter Twenty

Mia

"WHERE IS HE?" I CALLED to Kline, over the sound of the gunfire that rippled through the air in the living room. Kline shook her head, reloaded her gun, jaw set tight and mouth in a hard line.

"I don't know," she replied. "But we have to clear out this hallway before we go any farther."

"Right," I murmured, and I clutched the gun tighter in my hand. I hadn't had to use it yet, and I was hoping that I wasn't going to have to now. I could still remember how painful it had been to pull the trigger against the man on the highway, the one who had been going for Gabriel. Kline had pushed me down behind a pillar for cover while she and the rest of her men had been quick to clear out as much of the attacking forces as possible, but I knew that the chances of me getting out of there without having to fire a shot were slim to none.

Suddenly, I heard a noise—footsteps rushing by me, toward the corridor that led to my father's study.

"Where are they going," I muttered to myself. They weren't my father's men, I was sure of it—and then, I heard one of them shout to the others, and my stomach dropped in my chest.

"It's Hallow, he's in the study!"

Oh for shit's sake, Gabriel. My heart skipped several beats in my chest at the sound of his name, and it took an instant for me to work out what I had just heard. But this was happening. This was really happening.

"Kline!" I called to her. "He's in the study!"

"Get down there," Kline told me, as she ducked down behind the pillar once more. "We'll hold off as much as we can down here, but I can't promise anything. We don't have a lot of time."

"I'm going," I told her, and I squeezed her hand for a moment before I dived down the corridor to do as she had told me. I was hoping that my knowledge of the place would be enough to give me the upper hand, even if I didn't know how the hell someone like me was going to be able to fight my way out of there. I needed to run as far and as fast as I could, to get to that office before anyone else did, but I was already behind at least a half dozen of Tyrell's men, and I knew that the odds were against me.

I stuck to the walls, ducking behind pillars, sprinting between them as fast as I could and praying that nobody was going to look over their shoulder and see me running in behind them. I needed to keep moving. He was here, he was so close to me. I didn't know what they intended to do with him when they got him, but I sure as shit wasn't going to stand around waiting to find out.

The office door at the end of the corridor was busted open, and a small cluster of men already surrounded it. Was he still in there? I wasn't sure, right up until the moment I saw one of the men go to the door and be taken down by a few well-placed bullets from inside. Oh, yeah, he was still in there. Nobody but Gabriel could have taken out someone with that level of calm and confidence.

He was alive. I wanted to scream out to him, to tell him that I was right there, but I knew that I had to hold out a little longer. I prayed that I was going to be able to get to him before anyone else did. If I had to stand here and watch him die—I wasn't sure that I could have handled it. I knew that I had come this far, and that nothing was going to slow me down or stop me from doing what I needed to do.

I moved toward the office door as quietly as I could, hoping that I would be lost among the small group of men who had come down here to try and capture him. It said so much about Gabe's reputation that even this miniature army probably wouldn't have been enough to take him out for sure. He could have taken them all on at once and come out the other side in one piece. He was my man, and he would fight till the end to take what he knew he needed.

By the time I had managed to get close enough to the door, he had picked off another five, maybe six of the men trying to make their approach. I prayed that he was going to look out and check before he fired off another shot at me. I needed to see him again, I needed to speak to him, I needed to know that this was going to be okay. I needed to be certain that everything we had done for each other up until that point hadn't been for nothing, because I wasn't sure if I could have survived it if it wasn't.

Finally, finally, I saw him peer out from around the door. I gripped the gun tighter in my hands and felt the air break from my lungs for a moment as I looked at him. He had glanced in the wrong direction, so he wasn't going to see me standing there, but I didn't care. I would wait a lifetime if that's what it took for him to see me once more. And then ... and then—

He turned to me, and as soon as our eyes met, I felt a rush of relief course through my system. He smiled, even though I could tell he was in pain. His face was bruised and marked with cuts from some kind of fight that he had been in, but he was still standing, and right now, that was all that I needed to see.

"Gabe." I sobbed, as I fell toward him. I threw my arms around him and pulled him close to me. I didn't care that we were still in danger. All that mattered was that he was here beside me right now, and that we were going to be able to get out of this place in one piece. If I just kept pushing. If I just held on to him with everything that I had. We had come through so much already, and there was so much more for us to survive yet, but as long as we had each other...

I heard footsteps at the other end of the corridor, and my eyes sprang open to see who was closing in on us. I prayed that it was Kline, checking that I had managed to get to Gabriel in one piece, but instead, and to my horror, I saw Tyrell standing there. A gun in his hand. A gun that he was raising to point directly at Gabriel's back.

"Gabe!" I shrieked, and I tried to push him out of the way. I didn't know what else to do. I needed to fight for him right now, but he was too heavy for me to move in one shove. Tyrell was lining the gun up, already looked exhausted, as though he had battled his way through the whole house and then some to get here.

I had no choice. I had to do this myself.

The next few seconds, time seemed to slow down a little. I pulled the gun upright, jumping in front of Gabriel so that I could obscure Tyrell's shot. I had no idea if he would still take me out given the chance or if he was tired of all the trouble that I had caused him.

I managed to level the gun at him, or at least, I thought I did, but when I pulled the trigger, the bullet flew to his left, missing him entirely. But it caused him to jerk with shock, so at least I watched as he missed Gabriel with his first attempt.

And it was then that I felt the rage begin to rise inside of me. I had come this far to be with the man that I loved, and I wasn't going to let anyone on earth take that from me. Least of all a man like Ransom Tyrell, a man who wasn't worth the shit on my fucking shoe. I fired again, this time sending the bullet careening over his right shoulder, as he brought the gun back up to face Gabriel once more.

And then, I fired off the last shot. And this one hit him. I watched with a mixture of horror and relief as his left shoulder jerked back and the gun fell out of his hand, a spray of blood coating the paint next to him as he dropped to his knees. I gasped, and felt the gun slip out of my hands. I hadn't expected to actually make contact. I had no idea what the hell I was going to do now that I had him on his knees, but as long as he had backed off, as long as he was down for the count, that was all that I cared about. I wanted him gone. I wanted Gabriel safe. And for now, that's just what I had.

"Mia," Gabe murmured to me, and he pulled me against him, cradling my head in his hand. And being with him again, even in the mess of everything that was happening, was enough. I closed my eyes and tried not to think about the arch of blood that had escaped from Tyrell as I had pulled off the shot. All that mattered was that I had managed to keep Gabe safe. And that we were back together again, at last. I had no idea how long it would be before something tried to pull us apart again, but for now, we had each other, and that was all that I cared about. I kissed his cheek and gripped hold of him right, even though I knew that I should have been more careful with his battered and broken body right now.

The gunfire from the main corridor was still raging, and I knew that it wouldn't be long until it started to spill down here again and I had to run with him once more. But I just wanted a moment, a second, something that was going to make me feel like all of this had been worth it—and that was what he was giving me right now. That moment. That moment of relief that I had needed since the moment Kline and I had come up with this plan to get him out of here.

Chapter Twenty-One

Gabriel

I SANK TO MY KNEES, trying to contain the pain that was arching through every inch of my system. At the end of the corridor, I could hear Tyrell mumbling something, but it was totally incoherent. Or maybe it was just that my ears were giving out now that I had started to give up.

"Gabe!" Mia murmured to me, and she dropped to the floor in front of me, cupping my face in her hands and forcing me to look at her. There she was, the woman who I had done all of this for in the first place—if there was any better reason for the pain I was in right now, then I had yet to find it. She grasped my sleeve and pressed her forehead to mine, and I could feel the tears leaking down her face.

"You need to get out of here," she told me as she pressed a hand to my cheek. "You're burning up—"

"I'll be okay," I tried to assure her, but another wave of pain and nausea hit me, and I winced painfully. She shook her head.

"No, you won't be," she replied. "We need to get you to a hospital. Come on, please, just stand up."

She tried to ease me to my feet, but I was having a hard time keeping upright and felt my legs begin to shake. Footsteps at the other end of the corridor alerted me to someone else's presence, and my head snapped up, ready to fight again. But instead of one of Tyrell's men, I saw Kline. She had a smear of blood over one cheek and a gun in her hand, but she was otherwise unhurt.

"Shit! There you are," she muttered and joined Mia in trying to pull me to my feet.

"You're heavier than I remember," she told me, and I tried to come up with a snarky retort and failed. My brain felt like it was shutting off, slowly, something beginning to inch down the back of my spine. Like lights switching off in an office building, fading out of existence.

"Shit," Kline muttered. "Did you find him like this?"

"Yeah," Mia replied. "Do you think he's going to be okay?"

"I don't know," she admitted, and Mia let out this little whimper that made my heart ache. I couldn't believe how much I had put the two of them through. It just wasn't fair. They should have left me here, they should have gotten out, but then, if I knew one thing about the women in my life, it was that they were stubborn enough to still be in it after everything I had put them through. They weren't about to change that now.

"Okay, we can get him out to the car and then I'll drive to the hospital," Kline promised Mia. I could tell that she was doing her best to keep the younger woman calm, but I had no idea if Mia was going to believe any of it from her. I wished that there was something that I could do, something that I could say, anything that would make this a little easier to handle, but right now, all I could do was try to keep my feet moving underneath me and make sure that I got out of there in one piece. I had no idea how much longer I had left right now, how long I would be able to stay on my feet without them giving out from underneath me, but I would keep moving, keep thinking, keep pushing as long as I could.

At the end of the corridor, as the two women marshaled me toward the door, I became vaguely aware of the sight of a body there in front of me. Tyrell. He wasn't moving. A spray of blood from his chest had painted the wall behind him, and his eyes were still open, like he were trying to give out a last order to anyone who could hear him.

But they were glossed-over and opaque, and I knew that every inch of life that had been left in him was long gone. Good. That's what he deserved. For everything he had tried to do to Mia, to her family, I hoped that he never moved again in his life.

"Was that you?" Kline asked Mia. I felt Mia nodding against me.

"I think so."

"That was a good shot," she remarked.

Mia didn't reply. I knew that, even though she must have been glad that he was out of the picture for good, she didn't want to have to kill anyone else if she could help it. My heart ached for her, knowing that she'd had to do it again even after what she had been through before. It wasn't fair, none of this was fair. I wished that she hadn't had to be caught up in any of this, but I didn't see how else I could fix it right now. All I could do was fight with every inch of strength that I had left to make sure that I was there to help her through the pain she was trying to navigate now. I loved her too much to let her face it alone. She needed me, and I was going to make sure that I proved to her that she would never have to doubt how willing I was to be there for her.

I wasn't even sure where we were in the house right now. I could see floors moving beneath me, walls around me, but that was about it. I knew that my time was running out, and I held on to Mia tight, trying to tell her every way that I could that the only reason I was still standing upright was because she was there beside me, and I knew that I could survive anything if she was there to help me through whatever remained of my life.

The smell of gunfire filled the air, and I wondered how many men were still standing. This place must have been a fucking bloodbath. I didn't know how Mia and Kline had gotten in here, but I doubted they had done it without an army all of their own to boot. I would have to find out every detail of how they had managed this as soon as we were out of there. They would fill me in over a couple of beers and we would marvel that we had managed to make it out of there in one piece at all, and I would be sure, surer than ever, that the people I'd chosen to keep in my life had been the right ones.

But that would require me getting out of there in one piece first. I had no idea if I was going to be able to do it, but I smelled the fresh air outside the front of the house, and I knew that we were getting close to getting free. I knew that it wouldn't be long until I escaped for good, until I got out of there and made it out alive. And then ... and then...

"Stop right there."

My stomach dropped as soon as I heard that voice. I knew who it belonged to before we even turned around. But when I faced him, I still felt that swell of dread hitting me full force.

Sal.

He had a gun leveled at all three of us. The two women were doing their best to keep me upright and I knew that they couldn't reach for their weapons. If they even moved their hands, he would fire off a shot, and there wouldn't be anything he could do.

"Give me Hallow," he ordered Kline and Mia. They didn't move. He sighed, and this time, cocked the gun pointedly.

"Give me Hallow or I'm going to take all of you out right now." He growled at me.

The women still didn't let go of me. I almost wanted to tell them to give it up, that there was no point dying for my sake, but I knew that they would never have listened to me anyway. They were stubborn as hell, just the same way that I was, and even looking down the barrel of a gun of someone like Sal, they would never have backed off.

"Is that...?" Mia breathed, and I nodded.

"Sal, you don't have to do this," I tried to reason with him. "You can just walk out of here right now. You know that you're outnumbered, even if you take me out, you're not going to walk out of here alive—"

"And what makes you think I give a fuck about walking out of here alive?" he demanded. I could see that manic glint in his eye, and I knew that there was no way in hell that he was going to let me out of there without a bullet buried in my chest.

"Let go of him," he told the women once more. "Let go of him and I'll let the two of you live."

"I'm not going anywhere," Mia shot back at him, though I could hear her voice shaking. I knew that she wouldn't run, even if I had told her to, even if I had begged her.

"Your son is gone," I told Sal bluntly. "This isn't going to bring him back. The only way that—"

"I know he's gone." He snarled to me, his voice laced with such a fury that it made my chest ache. I knew that he had to be suffering in ways that I couldn't even have imagined, and I felt awful that I had been the one to do this to him. That I had been the one to pull the trigger on that man. Even though he had deserved it, for the way that he had laid his hands on Mia, his father would never recover from that pain, and he was right, it was a pain that I had caused him. I couldn't make that go away, no matter how hard I might have tried. His son was gone, and he was never going to be able to forgive me for that, and I had no idea how I was meant to make things better right now. If I could even come close to telling him everything that he needed to hear.

"And you're going to pay for that," he replied. "Only choice you have is if you're going to take those two girls down with you. So, Gabe, what's it going to be? You going to make them pay for what you did too?"

I caught my breath. I knew that if I told them to run, they would ignore me. That was the pain in the ass about having such loyal friends, even when you wanted them gone, they would make sure that they didn't go anywhere.

"I'm not leaving," Mia replied, and she tightened her grip around my waist. I knew that she was telling the truth. I could have begged and pleaded and told her that I wanted her to leave more than anything in the world and she still would have stood there at my side, defiant, making sure that everyone knew that I belonged to her. She hadn't come this far to back down now, and she wasn't going to stop when she knew that she had come so close to getting me out of there alive.

"Fine." He snarled back at us. And he lifted the gun, then paused for a moment as he looked between Kline, Mia, and me. These women who had saved my ass. I knew that I would never have been able to make it out of there if it hadn't been for them, and I was more grateful for that than I would ever be for anything else. They had believed in me enough, trusted me enough to come after me, even when it looked hopeless. No matter what happened next, I knew that I was grateful for that.

I watched as his finger tightened on the trigger, and I braced myself for the impact. I heard the *bang*, closed my eyes, and waited for the pain to come. I knew, at least, that I would be the one he took out first, and maybe that would give Kline and Mia enough time to run...

But the pain didn't come. And I lifted my head, slowly, to see Sal falling to his knees in front of us, his eyes glazed just the same way that Tyrell's had been. And behind him stood the man who had just managed to save our lives.

Chapter Twenty-Two

Mia

AS SAL SLUMPED TO THE floor in front of us, I stared at my father, who was still holding the gun that he just used to take out the other man. Smoke was curling from the tip, and it seemed to hang in the air for a long moment as though it was catching its breath.

Gabriel's weight was even heavier on my shoulders now, and I knew that the shock of everything we had just been through was too much for him to take. He started to fall to the floor, and Kline and I did our best to awkwardly maneuver him down without hurting him too badly.

"Shit," my father muttered, and he strode over to join us and get a look at how bad the damage might have been. I stared at my dad for the first time, properly, and saw a swelling under his eye, a slight limp to his posture. It was clear that he had been battling for his life just the same way that all of us had. But he didn't look as though he had anything on his mind but making sure that he got Gabriel out of there in one piece.

"We need to get him to a hospital," he announced, as he reached over to plant a hand against Gabe's neck. There were bruises starting to form on his skin, and I wondered just how recently he had been attacked. I had no idea what we were dealing with here, only that Gabe's eyes were becoming unfocused around the edges and I didn't know what else I could do to keep him with me right now.

"Gabe, please," I murmured, and I reached down to touch his cheek. For the briefest moment, his eyes met mine, and I knew that there was still enough of him left in that moment to save him.

"My men have secured the area," my father told me. "We can call in an ambulance—"

"That's going to take too long," I replied, shaking my head. "We need to get him out of here now. You must have something we can use to get him there?"

"I'll clear out one of the vans," he agreed. And, for the first time since I had found out about what he had planned for me and Tyrell, I felt like my father and I were on the same side. I knew that there was still so much for me to forgive him for, that it would be a long time before I could even come close to trusting him again, but for now, right here, in this moment, I was certain that I needed him, and I was certain that everything that he could do for me was going to keep Gabe alive.

"Won't the hospital be too dangerous?" Kline asked fretfully.

I turned to her. "What do you mean?"

"They'll have questions," she replied, shaking her head. "And if they see the state he's in, they're going to know what happened down here. I promised my men—"

"They won't have questions," my father snapped back to her, cutting her off.

It was almost funny, actually, since I knew that the two of them would probably have gotten along well if they hadn't been on opposite sides of the fence right now. I knew that Kline was right to worry, but she didn't know just how much influence my father had in this town—she had nothing to worry about, and I knew that he was going to do everything that he could to make sure that the cops didn't come poking around.

"They will," she replied. "I've dealt with this before, even if they patch him up at first, they're going to send people in to try to find out what put him in this state in the first place. And if that comes back to me, I'm going to land my brother and everyone who came out here to save him in trouble that I promised I was going to keep them out of. I'm not going to—"

"You don't have to do anything," my father told her, and I could tell that he was having to fight to keep his temper with her right now. She didn't understand just how much power he held in this town, though I was sure it wasn't going to take her long to figure it out. She didn't know everything that he had done over the years to keep himself safe, to make sure that the people who worked for him did exactly what he wanted them to. He promised a certain level of security to everyone who worked for him, and nothing was going to change that.

Gabe groaned, and I planted a hand on his chest to make sure that his heart was still beating. I couldn't believe this was happening. I knew why Kline was scared, but couldn't she see how much pain he was in? How close he was to falling over the edge that we couldn't bring him back from?

"Isn't there a doctor here?" she asked. "On the property?"

"He's gone," Gabe muttered. "I told him to leave. He tried to help me—"

He caught his breath again and I smoothed his matted hair back from his head.

"You don't have to say anything," I promised him softly. "We've got you, all right? We've got you."

"If we don't get him to a hospital in the next hour, he's going to die," my father argued with Kline angrily.

"And what happens then?" she demanded. "If the police turn up—"

"I'll call ahead and make sure they have no reason to," he assured her. She didn't sound convinced. I was still stroking Gabe's face. His skin was burning up, hot and clammy, and I didn't know how much time we had left. If these two stripped the last moments of his life by arguing about what the best course of action was for him, then I would—

"You really think you can just get the cops to drop it like that?" Kline demanded.

I could hear my father getting more and more pissed with every passing second, but he was trying, at least, to soothe her before she blew her top.

"I know I can," he replied. "I've done it before. I'll do it again. I've already lost one son this week, I'm not going to lose another just because you're worried about your men."

His son? Had he really just called Gabe his son? I looked down at the man before me, the man who I loved so much it made my chest hurt, and I wondered if he had heard that part. I prayed that he had. I knew that he must have been delirious, nearly out of it by now, but even just a hint of something that promised him he was still part of this family might have made the difference.

"I'm going to get a car," my father announced.

Kline stepped in front of him. "Can you guarantee—"

"I can guarantee that Gabe is going to die if you don't let me do what has to be done!" he roared to her, finally losing his temper.

I didn't blame him. I knew that Kline meant well, but she was pushing her luck far too close to the edge for my liking. Gabriel was running out of time right before us, and she was arguing about the details of how she was going to keep her men safe.

"I'm going to call ahead to the hospital now," he told her sharply. "You bring a car around and find some men who are strong enough to get Gabriel into it."

He took a step toward her and narrowed his eyes at her. It was about the first and only time I had ever seen Kline look anything close to scared in the entire time that I had known her, and I wasn't surprised. My father could be seriously intimidating if he wanted to be, and now, it seemed, he wanted nothing more than to have this woman crumple and give in to what he was telling her.

"I am more powerful than anyone else in this city," he told her, without leaving an inch of room for argument. "And I will not be told what to do by anyone else. If I want to get him to a hospital, I am going to get him to a hospital, and I am going to make sure that nobody there looks twice at him, do you understand?"

Kline eyed him for a moment, and then looked over at Gabriel. I gazed up at her, imploring her to do the right thing here. She knew that we hadn't come this far to fail now, not when he needed us so badly. He was running out of time, and we needed to get him somewhere safe, somewhere that they could keep him alive.

"Fine," she replied. Her voice was taut and edged with irritation, but I didn't care. All that mattered to me right now was the certainty that she was going to give us what we needed. She strode out of the front door of the house and left my father and me alone with Gabriel once more.

He came to kneel down at Gabe's side again, and this time, he reached out to touch his shoulder.

"We're going to get you somewhere safe," he promised him, though he must have known as well as I did that Gabe couldn't hear much of anything. I looked over at my father, and for the first time in longer than I could remember, I felt relief that he was the man who had brought me into this world. He might have hated a lot of what I had done these last few weeks, but he still loved me enough to want to keep alive the man who he knew I loved. It might not have been much, but it was something, and something was enough to keep my head above water for the time being. "Something" was everything that I needed right now.

"Thank you." I breathed to him, and he didn't take his eyes off Gabriel, his mouth tight and his eyes full of doubt.

"You don't have anything to thank me for yet," he told me sharply.

I knew that the harshness in his tone wasn't aimed at me, but I didn't care about it, anyway. I had been through enough, seen enough these last few years, to be able to let go of whatever doubt still clung to me right now. Whether or not he accepted me or what I had chosen to do, I knew that I could stand on my own two feet. If not for myself, then for Gabriel, who had made me promise to him that I was never going to stop fighting.

And all I asked from him now was that he gave me the same thing in return. I knew that it was going to be hard for him to fight every step of the way, but that's all I needed from him right now. Things had been hard enough, life had thrown so many obstacles in our way since we had first fallen for each other, but it was all going to start changing now. Just as soon as we got out of this particular mess, we were going to be able to be together, and as soon as that happened, well, I knew that all of this would fade into obscurity. Nothing else would matter as long as he was there by my side.

And he just had to hold on a little longer before I knew that we could be together for good. I took his hand and squeezed it tight and sent every inch of healing energy I had to him. Because I needed him to live. And there was no way in hell I was letting him slip through my fingers now.

Chapter Twenty-Three

Gabriel

WHEN I CAME TO, IT was to a sharp stab of pain in my side, and the reminder that, whether I liked it or not, I was alive.

Distantly, I could hear the sound of a beeping monitor, but it took me a second to actually work out where that was coming from. I winced and peeled myself upright on the bed, inhaled the scent of the sterile hospital around me, and tried to work out just how long I had been out of it.

But there was one thing that drew my attention before anything else. And that was the woman, fast asleep on the seat next to me. She had her forearms against the bed, her face smushed up against the back of her hand, and she was breathing slowly as she slept.

Mia. I reached over to touch the back of her head, feeling her soft hair beneath my fingers and knowing with a sureness that everything was going to be all right. She was right there beside me, and that meant that I was going to be able to make it through anything that this day might have thrown at me. She was still wearing the same clothes that she'd had on when I had seen her the last time, and I doubted that she had gotten much rest since then.

Slowly, she stirred, and when she saw me looking at her, she snapped her head up, eyes wide and shining with relief.

"Gabe!" she exclaimed. "You're awake..."

"I sure am," I replied, wincing as I tried to adjust myself a little. "Though I think I might be better off asleep right now, to be honest."

"Does it hurt a lot?" She fussed over me, rising to her feet and adjusting the pillow at my back.

"Yes, but it could be a hell of a lot worse," I replied, and she nodded at once.

"Tell me about it," she agreed. "I thought you were, well, let's just say that it was pretty touch-and-go there for a hot second. I wasn't sure that I was going to get you out of there in one piece."

"I wouldn't have made it if it wasn't for you," I told her, and she smiled at me.

"And my father," she reminded me. "And Kline. And everyone from your old life that she managed to get together to come help you fight your way out."

"Yeah, that too," I agreed, and I felt a sharp stab of pain running down the side of my face. I reached up to touch it, to apply some pressure to the wound, but I just found a clean dressing against it instead.

"You need to lay off." She reached up to brush my hand away from my face.

"How bad is it?" I asked her.

She shook her head. "It's hard to tell right now, but the doctors said they thought you had a pretty good chance of making a full recovery—"

"I was talking about my face," I corrected her, and she laughed.

"Well, there's not much we can do about that," she teased. "But I'm sure you'll be back to your usual self soon enough." She frowned for a moment, though, as she looked at me.

"I can't believe what a number Sal did on you," she murmured, as she took my hand and squeezed it softly. "I wish I could have gotten there sooner. If I had just—"

"If you had come there any sooner, I might not have been out of the room he was holding me in yet," I pointed out to her, and she lowered her gaze to the ground and nodded.

"I get it," she replied. "But I just wish I could have saved you all that pain. It's not fair that you had to go through that."

"Me too," I agreed. "But it's worth it to see you again."

She leaned down to plant a kiss on the back of my hand, and laid her head gently against it for a moment. With her eyes closed, she continued to speak, as though what she had to say was too painful for her to even think about saying while she looked into my eyes.

"I thought I'd lost you," she admitted. "There was a second there, before we got you to the hospital, I thought you were gone. And I didn't know what the hell I was going to do with myself."

"You're going to have to try a little harder than that to get rid of me," I replied, trying to lighten the mood, but when she looked up at me, her eyes were glistening with tears.

"I mean it," she confessed. "I couldn't—I don't know what I would do with myself if I lost you, Gabe."

"You don't have to think about that anymore," I promised her, and I leaned over to kiss her, to try and comfort some of the tears away from her cheeks. But, as I moved, I felt a stab of pain in my side, and I winced.

"You need to rest," she told me.

"So do you," I shot back. "You haven't changed out of those clothes all day—"

"All night," she corrected me, making a face. "You were out for nearly twenty-four hours."

"Dammit," I muttered. "And you've been here all alone?"

"Kline came by a few times, but I didn't really know what to say to her," she admitted. "So she left again."

"She's never been great with the emotional stuff," I agreed. "She helped you with the attack on the house?"

"She got her brother and a bunch of other people together so that we could take it," she replied, unable to keep the smile off her face. "I didn't think that it was actually going to work, but when we got there my father was already starting on the place, so we just worked together. Tyrell didn't even know what hit him—"

Her face suddenly dropped, as though she had just remembered what exactly had happened to Tyrell, just what she had done to him. I didn't even want to think about how much it must have been paining her right now, having taken his life. But I knew she had done the right thing. The world was a much better place without him in it, and now she didn't have to worry about that motherfucker trying to make an example of her or her family any longer.

"You did the right thing," I promised her, and she managed to look up at me again. As soon as her eyes locked with mine, a small smile spread over her face, and she nodded.

"Yeah," she replied. "I think I did."

She let out a huge yawn and slumped back into the chair next to my bed, clearly exhausted, still holding my hand.

"You should go home," I told her. "You need to get some rest—"

"I'm not going anywhere till you're on your feet again," she replied.

"Have you even eaten anything since you got here?" I asked her.

She shrugged. "I honestly can't remember," she replied, then yawned again. "Kline said she was going to get me something for breakfast, but I'm not sure how long she's going to be."

She leaned down to kiss the back of my hand again, and this time, she smiled up at me as though she couldn't have been happier in that moment.

"Gabe," she murmured, and I locked eyes with her. It felt so good not to have to scramble to try and look at her like I had done before. My brain felt more focused now, and being here with her, everything seemed to take on a pinpoint accuracy.

"I love you," she told me. I had been waiting a long time to hear those words come out of her mouth, to hear them again in person, at least. To hear them without knowing that we might never get a chance to say them out loud to each other ever again. I had no idea how long it had been since I had said the words to her last, but there were never too many times to tell her the truth of how I felt.

"I love you too," I replied, and she moved toward me so that I could kiss her on the lips without sending a start of pain through my abdomen once more. And as soon as our mouths met, I knew that it had been worth it. Not just what had put me in the hospital, but everything that had led to this moment—everything that had happened to get me here, to leave me alone with her once more. Everything that I had given up and all the ways that I had changed just to make sure that I came out the other side feeling like a brand-new person. She was worth it. I had never doubted it, but if I ever needed confirmation, this was it.

She brushed her nose against mine as she pulled back, and she smiled so wide it looked as though it was going to split her face in two.

"I can't wait till you're feeling all the way better," she remarked suggestively, letting her hand trace up my arm for a moment. Even though I was in so much pain, I couldn't help but feel that pulse of want for her, for everything that she could give to me. No matter how much I might have tried to deny it, there was always going to be chemistry there, even when I felt as though I'd had the shit recently and comprehensively kicked out of me.

"Oh, you're awake!" a voice exclaimed from the doorway, and we both looked around to see Kline making her way toward us. She was carrying an armful of food, much to my relief, and I was glad to see that she seemed as concerned about taking care of Mia as I did.

"It's so good to see you upright, buddy," she remarked, as she stepped through the doorway and handed Mia a coffee and a bagel. She passed me a cup, too, though she pressed her finger to her lips.

"I'm pretty sure you're not meant to be having this, so don't say anything, okay?" she ordered me.

I nodded at once. "You have my word," I replied, and I smiled as I took a sip of the drink. Now, that was what I had been waiting for.

"How are you feeling?" she asked me, as Mia took a bite of her bagel and tucked her legs up underneath herself.

"Not great, but I'll be better soon," I assured her. She grinned at me and nodded.

"That's the attitude I'm talking about!" she exclaimed. She seemed a little hyper, and I wondered just how much anxiety she had been running on all night to stay with Mia. I was grateful for everything that she had done to take care of the woman I loved, and I knew that I owed her my life just as much as I did Mia. The two of them had pulled together nothing short of a miracle to get me out of there.

And now, I was out the other side alive, and as well as I could be given what had happened. It was a relief that I would never get over, everything that they had done, and I was glad that I had the two of them to rely on. But, more than anything, I was glad that I had a woman like Mia on my side. A woman as fierce, as bold, as brilliant, and as loving as she was. As long as I had her, everything else would fall into place.

Chapter Twenty-Four

Mia

"HEY, CAREFUL," I WARNED Gabe, as I helped lead him through the door and into the living room of the small condo that I was sharing with Jasmine for the time being.

"I feel like that's all anyone has said to me the last week." He grumbled, but I knew that it was good-natured. He had been through enough to know that people were going to be fussing over him for the foreseeable future, and he didn't actually seem too mad about it. I wondered how long it had been since he had just allowed someone to take care of him, instead of having to be the one in charge.

But for now, I was going to be the one taking care of him, and I intended to make certain that he knew that he was my patient. I had been in and out of the hospital the last ten days, making sure that he was making a full recovery, and it had been exhausting—the trip from Jasmine's condo all the way to the hospital and back again was way longer than it ever should have been, but I would have made it a million times over if it meant that I got the chance to see him every day.

He had been improving pretty well since he had been brought in, some of the wounds and cuts on his body healing up. Every day, I would sit there next to his bed and look at him, take in every inch of his body, the body that he had put on the line to make sure that I was safe no matter what. And I promised myself that I was never going to forget how this felt, seeing him this way, seeing what he had been through. I

146

would be forever grateful for how far he had gone and how far I knew he was willing to go to give me everything that I needed.

And it was the least that I could give him back in return now that he was doing a little better. I wished that I could have brought him back somewhere a little fancier than this, but it wasn't like my father's mansion was an option, given that it was mostly rubble right now. Jasmine had been sweet enough to put me up in her place for a few days, and, when I had told her that I was going to be bringing Gabe back this evening, she had promised that she would clear out so we could have the place to ourselves.

I gently guided him to the couch, then went to drop off the medication and other shit that the hospital had sent him home with. My father had insisted on paying for every expense that he had incurred, and I wasn't going to argue. Wasn't like either of us were exactly rolling cash ourselves, was it? Not until I managed to find a job for myself doing something vaguely useful, and I had no idea how long that was going to take.

I tried my best not to think about it. I just had to focus on the fact that he was here with me right now. And that he was in one piece, something that I didn't think I would ever get to say about him and mean it.

He lay down on the couch, and I planted myself next to him once I had stashed away all his stuff. I knew that he was going to need me to fuss over him, and I was looking forward to doing just that.

"How are you doing?" I asked him, and he smiled at me.

"I'm glad you're here to look after me," he explained, and I smiled right back at him.

"Me too," I agreed. "Do you need any meds? Anything like that?"

"Are you going to be this controlling the whole time I'm here?" He laughed, and I tipped my head to the side playfully.

"Oh, you're saying it like it's a bad thing," I replied. "I'm going to be in control, and you're going to like it, you hear me?"

"I don't think I have much of a choice," he murmured, and he reached for me. I slid my hands down over his arms and pushed them back against the couch playfully. Even though he could have tossed me off in an instant, even in his weakened state, he grinned right back at me.

I leaned down to kiss him properly. He parted his lips at once and pushed his tongue into my mouth, and I snuggled down against him happily. Damn, I had been waiting so long for this moment that it was hard to believe that it was really here. I knew that he wanted me, I knew that the two of us had been starving-hungry for each other the whole time that we had been in the hospital. Every moment that I had been able to steal with him was so sweet and so torturous at the same time, because I wanted nothing more than to strip him naked and fuck him on the spot.

I slowly began to peel open his shirt, taking my time and going slow to make sure that I didn't cause any unnecessary pain to his wounds and dressings. He didn't even wince, kissing me a little harder, keeping his hands where I had left them as though he was game to play by my rules for a while. It was the first time we had ever really done something like that, and I had to admit, there was something seriously sexy to me about the thought of everything that I could do to him right now—all the ways that I could get my hands on him, everything that I could use this gorgeous body for.

I kissed down his neck and over his strong chest, taking my time, letting him get used to the closeness of my body to his once more. I knew that the two of us had been to hell and back, and I felt like it was only fair that we got to experience a little more of heaven, right?

Moving my hand down between his legs, I squeezed his impressive erection, and couldn't help but let out a little moan of delight as I felt how hard he was in that moment.

"Mmm." I purred in his ear. "I think you have something that Nurse Mia needs to take care of."

I couldn't help but giggle at how cheesy the words sounded coming out of my mouth, but he didn't seem to care. After all the time we had been waiting to do this, I supposed that he was just glad to have me ready, willing, and squirming around on top of him right now.

I unzipped his pants slowly and slipped my hand into his underwear, wrapping my fingers around his erection and parting my lips with a delighted little gasp as I felt him against my skin. Damn, how had I been able to resist him for so long? I knew that he had been a bedridden until now, but even still ... the feel of his hardness in my hand was enough to send this surge of want through me that, for a second, rendered me helpless. I had to catch my breath to pull myself back to that moment and reminded myself that I was meant to be the one in control.

I slipped down his pants and kissed him again, tucking my hand behind his head so that I could really show him how much I wanted him. Stroking his cock as I ground my hips against his leg, I listened for that deep growl that he let out to tell me that he was enjoying every single little thing that I was doing right now.

"You want to be inside me, Gabe?" I murmured to him, letting my lips tease at his lobe for a moment. He reached and sank his fingers on my ass, pushing me roughly against him.

"Right now." He growled back at me. And I knew that he wasn't going to take no for an answer.

I pulled my panties down and pushed up the skirt that I had been wearing—I had known that I wasn't going to be able to last long without fucking him after we came through the door, and I had assumed, rightly, it seemed, that stripping down to the bare minimum was the best that I could do right now. Shifting so that I could push against him playfully, I tugged his underwear down to release his cock and continued to pump my hand against his erection. Damn, he looked so big against me like that. He must have noticed the difference. Sometimes, I wondered how in the name of holy hell I had ever been able to fit something that big all the way inside of me, but as I climbed on top of him, spreading my legs to straddle him, I felt my pussy aching for him, and I knew that it wasn't going to be a problem.

Slowly, slowly, slowly, I lowered myself down on top of him, gripping his base to hold him in place as I rolled my hips down to take him. I groaned loudly—it was the first time he had been inside of me in way too long for my liking, and the sensation was so impossibly, erotically delicious that I could hardly contain it. I was glad that Jasmine wasn't here, because I doubted she would have gotten any sleep with us in the building tonight.

His hands came to my hips to hold me steady for a moment, and I opened my eyes and looked down at him—my man, his face written with a helpless desire that I had put there for him. And with that, I started to move my hips, making the very most of this that I possibly could, and losing myself to how good it felt to have him right back where he belonged once more.

His fullness was satisfying in a way that nothing else ever had been, in a way that I was sure nothing else ever could be to me. As I tipped my head back, grasping hold of his hands again for leverage because I knew that his chest would be too tender for that, I couldn't contain the rush of this. I had wanted this for so long that I had almost forgotten how good the reality of it could be. He was perfect, his body made for mine as much as mine had been made for his.

"You look perfect like that." He breathed to me, and I smiled down at him and allowed him to slide his arms around my waist and pull me against him once more. He thrust up and into me, still strong enough to fill me the way that I needed to be filled, and I closed my eyes and just reveled in how delicious it was to have him right where I wanted him. To be here, where he needed me.

It didn't take long till I could feel myself getting close to the edge. I had been waiting so long for this, and now it was here, happening, all that tension building so fast I couldn't control it. I tipped my head back and sat back up on him, pushing myself down as hard as I could—and felt my pussy clench roughly around him over and over again. I cried out, the sound ripping out of me, and then, moments later, I felt his warm seed inside of me, the addiction that had gone unaddressed filled finally once more.

And with that, I flopped down on top of him, and planted a kiss right against his heart. I could feel it beating hard against his chest, and I knew that, just like me, this was everything he had been waiting for.

Chapter Twenty-Five

Gabriel

AS I WATCHED MIA STUFF the last of her clothes into her suitcase, I couldn't help but wonder if she was rushing into this.

"Are you sure you don't want to stay a little longer?" I asked her, and she shook her head as she tossed a couple of bikinis into her bag. They looked like they wouldn't have covered much more than the bare minimum, and I was looking forward to seeing her in them as soon as I got the chance.

"No, I need to get out of here," she replied, and I sat up on the couch so that I could face her properly. It had only been a week or so since I had come out of the hospital, but the wounds were already starting to heal themselves, and there was only pain if I shifted in the wrong direction or something.

"You could tell your father that you're going, at least," I pointed out, as gently as I could.

She fired a look in my direction. "I don't think that's a good idea," she admitted with a sigh. "Not until I work out what I actually want from this."

"I get it," I agreed. "But I thought you already knew what you wanted, right?"

I pointed my thumb at myself, and she shook her head and giggled.

"You know, you're lucky you're so cute, because if not, you'd be a totally arrogant asshole," she replied, and I reached out to pull her down next to me. She planted herself on the couch beside me and let out a yawn, letting her head rest against my shoulder for a moment.

"I just need some time to figure out what I want," she admitted, and I smoothed her hair back from her head and nodded. I knew what she meant.

"I know," I agreed, and I kissed her on the forehead. "I know, baby."

It's strange to think that we were going to be moving on again so soon, but I supposed Jasmine must have been glad that she was going to get this condo back to herself. It was hardly enough room for all three of us, and we had probably been getting in her way all this time, though she's far too sweet to say anything about it. Where exactly we were going, I wasn't sure, but Mia had cashed in the last of her inheritance to make sure that we would have plenty to survive on.

She still hadn't told her father that we were planning to leave the country for a while, but honestly, I get why she didn't want him to find out the truth about it. He had already been through enough these last few weeks, and he was trying to right himself after the chaos that had nearly ripped his life to pieces right in front of him. I hardly blamed her for wanting to cut him some slack, even if I wasn't sure that he entirely deserved it, after what he had almost done to her.

"Have you told Kline that we're leaving?" I asked Mia, and she nodded.

"Yeah, she said it was good riddance," she replied with a chuckle. "I think she'll be glad to see the back of us. We caused her way more trouble than she'd had to deal with in a while."

"Yeah, and she's got plenty enough to keep her busy now," I agreed. Ever since the attack on the Romano house, Kline had basically stepped in to cover for Donnie's death, taking control of the men that he had left behind and giving them some guidance so that they could make some sense of their new lives going forward. I knew that she would do good things with them, better things than Donnie had ever thought to do, but it wasn't what she had expected to be doing with her life, and

I wouldn't have blamed her if she was dealing with a little shock at the shift that her life had taken since we'd come into it.

"As long as she has her dogs, she'll be fine," Mia replied. "And I'll make sure to bring her back a big bottle of something alcoholic from wherever we end up."

"Sounds good to me," I agreed, and she wrapped her arms around my waist carefully. I kept telling her that she didn't have to worry about hurting me anymore, but she still touched me as though she did. I knew that it was going to be a long time before she got out of that habit, but I couldn't blame her for that. After everything that we had been through, she was always going to want to play it safe with me, and I wasn't going to go arguing with it.

"I'm sure that'll make it up to her," she agreed, and she stared off into space for a moment, the corners of her mouth turning downward. I knew that she must have had a thousand thoughts running through her mind in that instant. A thousand questions as to what the hell she was going to do next and what her life was going to look like now that she had so much to handle.

In some ways, I supposed, it had been easier for her when we had been on the run together. Because at least we'd had something to stay focused on then. At least the conflicts that she felt were reduced down to just the push and pull of whether we were going to make it through the night. Not like this ... not like it was now, when everything seemed to go spiraling into a mess that I couldn't make sense of.

We had to work out what we were going to do next with our lives. And that was the hard part. With nobody chasing us down, with nobody out to kill us, there had to be something that we did to fill in the gaps now, but I had no idea what the hell that was supposed to be, and, judging by the way she had reacted to all of this, too, I would say that she felt much the same way that I did.

"Are you worried about your father?" I asked her bluntly. I knew that he had to be on her mind right now, after everything that he had lost. After his son had slipped through his fingers, not to mention the home that he had built for his family for all those years. But she shook her head.

"Glo's there with him right now," she pointed out. "And she can handle herself. If anyone's stupid enough to try and come after him now, I'd bet that she'll take them out before they can even get close. He'll be fine."

"I wasn't just talking about his physical safety," I replied, as gently as I could.

She sighed. "I know that," she admitted. "But I can't sit around trying to take care of him for the rest of my life. I need to know what's right for me. I spent so long just trying to do what was right for him, what was right for the family, and I don't—I'm not—willing to give up on finding out what really works for me yet. I have a lot to figure out."

"Like whether you're going to go back to be with the family, or strike out on your own?" I replied.

She nodded. "Yeah, something like that," she agreed. "It's just..." She trailed off.

I knew what she was thinking. There was so much to be said, so much to think about, that she didn't even know where to start.

In truth, though, I was pretty sure that she already knew what she wanted for herself going forward. She might not have been too keen to admit it, but I wouldn't have been surprised if she decided that she wanted to go back to the family after everything that she had been through. It wasn't that she couldn't have handled the hard stuff if she had to—I had already seen her work her way through more than most people would have to face up to in a lifetime—but that she *didn't want* to have to deal with it.

And, honestly, that was the way I wanted it too. I had always believed that I was only good for one thing, for delivering whatever the people I worked for wanted from me. But now, with her, I could see that there was more to me than I had ever believed there could be. And

I wasn't going to round back on that and return to what I had been before, not if I could help it. Whatever she wanted from me, I would be there, at her side, without a doubt, but I was quite sure that I already knew what she desired. She just had to take some time to herself to work it out, once and for all. And I was going to be there every step of the way.

She got to her feet to start packing again and cocked her head to the side to look at me for a moment.

"Don't you have your own clothes to be packing?" she asked me.

I shook my head. "Nothing much," I replied. "I don't think I'll be needing much in the way of clothes, anyway."

"Oh, and what's that supposed to mean?" she shot back playfully. "I hope you're not getting any ideas in your head, Hallow."

"Oh, I am," I replied, and I glanced at the bikinis that she had tossed into her suitcase. "Though they mostly revolve around getting you out of everything that you've put in there."

"You're filth, you know that?" She laughed, but she was clearly happy with our little flirtation. And I was happy to give her everything that she wanted right now. All that I needed in the world was to see her with that smile on her face and to know that I had been the one to put it there. To know that she was starting to detach from all the stress and all the terror that had come from the place that we had been in before. I knew that we still had far to go before that was behind us for good, but as soon as it was, I was going to enjoy every second of it. And, before we got there, I was going to hold her hand and stand by her side for every inch of the long journey that we had ahead of us.

As she hummed to herself, continuing to pack, I just watched her. I never thought that we would get this part. I never thought I would be able to look at her and not have to worry about a bullet tearing through the window beside us, or the screech of a car announcing that someone was here to try and steal us away once again. I could just be at peace, with the woman who meant so much to me, and I was going to enjoy every single second of it that I could. I knew that we belonged together, and I knew that nothing on earth was going to change that. As long as she was by my side, everything else would fall into place. And I knew that whatever was to come next, we could handle it. Because we would be together. And that was all that I needed right now.

Chapter Twenty-Six

Mia

I WOKE TO THE SOUND of the waves lapping up the beach outside the house, and I smiled as I inhaled a great big lungful of the salty, clear air.

Beside me, Gabe was still sleeping. He had been restless on the flight over here, and I had told him to sleep in as long as he needed to now that we had arrived. This trip was about taking a break, stepping back, and affirming what we knew we both wanted, and I was going to make the very most of it that I possibly could.

Hawaii. There had only been one place in my mind when I pictured getting out of Chicago. Somewhere that would allow us to find the freedom from the cold winter and the memories that plagued us everywhere we turned. I needed the sun to burn off the memories, to burn off the reminders of everything that had happened to us. I never wanted to look back. If we could have just moved into this villa right now, I would have put down the deposit today.

But it was far too expensive for that. My father had insisted on paying for this trip for us, an attempt to atone for some of his sins. Not that it was enough for me to forgive him for everything, but I sure as hell wasn't going to go turning down the offer of a free break from reality for a while. The villa that he had paid for was beautiful, secluded, and had its own private beach that led to the crystalline blue waters below. They lapped right up against the balcony in the morning, and I intended to make the very most of it that I could.

I planted a kiss on Gabe's sleeping head and slipped out of bed so that I could look over the water below us. This place was perfect, really. I hadn't done enough traveling in my life, and I intended to do everything that I could to fix that now that I was finally out from under the thumb of my father at last. I was just glad that I had managed to get out of Chicago. It had felt as though there were weights pinning me down everywhere I moved there, even though it was full of people I loved and cared for—Kline, Jasmine, even Glo and my father, I supposed. But I needed to shake off everything that had happened, and the only way that I was going to be able to do that was getting as far from there as I possibly could.

The memory of my brother was too much for me to handle, sometimes. Even now, after spending a week or so out here, I found myself staring into the sea and thinking about him. Gabe had told me how he had died, in his arms, with my father at his side, and I was grateful that he'd had his friend there to guide him through everything. I knew that he would have hated the thought of being so vulnerable with someone else and not having something sharp and snarky to say about it, but I needed to know that he gone with someone who cared for him by his side.

And I thanked him, every night before I went to bed, for keeping Gabriel alive. I didn't know what I would have been doing if Gabe hadn't made it out of there in one piece. My mind would just shut off every time I tried to consider that eventuality, as though it refused to even consider that it could be true. I didn't blame it. Things were so perfect with us now that the thought of being without him stung far too deeply for me to bear. He was here, and that was all that mattered. He was here, and I was with him, and we had managed to get out of there alive, and sometimes, when I woke up in the middle of the night in a cold sweat with the sound of a gunshot ringing in my ears, that was all that I had to cling to.

But this morning, I felt peaceful. I had slept well, and the smell of the sea and the sand was too tempting to deny. I pulled off the shirt that I had slept in and headed, barefoot, toward the water, even though I knew that it would be cold at this time in the morning. Good. Nothing woke you up like a cold dip, right? I was pretty sure that some people in Iceland did this every morning, but with ice water. I would have to go down there myself to find out one of these days.

Taking a deep breath, I dived headfirst into the sea, letting the water swallow me up whole for a moment. And, instead of feeling scared or overwhelmed, I felt ... free. Something like it, anyway. I had been feeling that a lot lately, but it was such a shockingly new emotion to me that it had taken me a long time to figure out that was actually what was going through my mind. Strange to think that, after all those years, I had finally begun to understand what it actually meant to do things on my own terms. To live life for myself. Not for the people around me, not for what I thought they wanted from me. Just for me.

A girl could get used to this, that was for sure. I closed my eyes and flipped over under the water, coming up a few feet from the balcony once more and smiling at the clear blue sky above me. There was something safe about being cradled by the water like this, being held in this way, as though the earth itself was holding me against its chest and telling me that everything was going to be just fine. I wasn't sure that I believed it yet, not fully, but I was getting there, and that was more than could be said for the person I had been before.

"Well, good morning."

I looked up, and saw Gabe standing there on the balcony above me, leaning on the railing and looking down at me with a grin on his face. He was wearing only a pair of boxers, and he looked fine as hell. The bullet wound on his shoulder had started to fade now, and was a pale pink in color, far from the aggressive red that had marked it out before.

"Morning," I called back to him, pushing my hair back from my face and treading water to keep myself up. "You sleep well?"

"Better," he agreed, and he looked at my half-naked body under the water and grinned. "Better now that I've seen you."

"Enjoying the view?" I asked him, spinning around playfully in the water below him. He nodded.

"I sure am," he replied.

"Sorry for waking you up," I told him, making an apologetic face.

He shook his head. "Oh, it was worth it," he replied. "Trust me."

"Want me to come up there and make it even more worth it?" I asked him playfully. I wasn't kidding. I felt as though my libido had gone through the roof since we had landed out here together. There was something about the slowness of life in this place that made it way easier to switch myself on, to feel that attraction to him without guilt or second-guessing myself. I had spent such a long time trying not to worry about losing him, about what would happen if he slipped through my fingers, but I didn't have to think about that for another second. He was mine, all mine, and I was going to enjoy every single inch of his body every single way that he was going to let me.

He reached down to help me up on to the balcony, and the water dripped from my body to the wood below us. He grasped hold of my waist and looked me up and down, his hands strong and sure on my body as he held me.

"You know you're perfect, don't you?" he murmured to me, as he pulled me against his muscular form. I felt my breath catch in my throat. Was there ever going to be a time when this man didn't send tingles through my whole system? A time when I could resist the impossibly intense chemistry that always seemed to burn between us?

"Hmm, I could do with reminding." I purred to him playfully, just the moment before our lips met. He hitched me up from the ground and planted me on the bar behind me, the one that separated us from the sea beyond, and peeled off my sopping-wet panties from my body, letting them fall to the ground below us.

I wrapped my arms around him and kissed him back. I knew that I would have given anything for this moment to keep on going, to stretch out into eternity. Whenever we kissed, it was as though the world slowed to nothing and gave in to just the sweetness of his lips on mine, of the way his mouth felt as he kissed me deeply.

But he wasn't going to stop at just my mouth again. No, instead, he moved down to his knees, spreading my legs wide, and I gripped hold of his shoulders tightly, clinging on for dear life. One wrong move and I could go falling over the edge and into the ocean below us, and I knew he was about to make it very hard for me to stay focused right now.

"Mmm." He moaned softly, as he brushed his tongue up the inside of my thigh. I could already feel the warmth of his lips against the prickling coolness of my skin, and I looked down and watched him as he moved closer, closer, closer, and then—

"Fuck." I groaned, as his mouth finally found my pussy. His tongue swirled around my clit softly, and I had to catch my breath to keep myself from losing any sense of control in my body at all. He grabbed hold of my ass, pulling me on to him, and I arched my hips so that I could push them back on to him eagerly. He sealed his lips around my clit and began to suck softly, taking his time, going slow and letting me get used to it before he started to focus his attention more directly against me. I squirmed, the pleasure so delicious that it was making my head spin even though he had just started.

But this was how it always was with him. Being with him like this, it was always a gift—being with him in this way was always enough to make my body forget all the pain that it had gone through, all the wounds that it was carrying, even if they were only on the inside. I balled my hands in his hair and let a cry escape my lips as I focused on the sheer decadence of the sensation that came from his mouth, as he started to lap at me with a soft tongue designed to make my toes curl helplessly. How did he always know just what I wanted?

It didn't take long till I could feel that stirring inside of me, that promise that he was still just as good as he had ever been at making me come. I knew that I could have done this a thousand times over with him, and it would never have grown old—as long as he was the one here by my side, nothing else mattered, and I was going to hold on to that as the only certainty in the mess that had become of my life these last few months.

But maybe a mess is what I had needed. Because it was a mess that had led me to here, with him. And, as I tipped my head back and let the orgasm grow inside of me, I knew that it was where I needed to be right now. Where I had always needed to be. And nothing ... nothing was going to change that.

Chapter Twenty-Seven

Gabriel

I FELT HER THIGHS CLENCH around my head, a sure sign that she was close, and, sure enough, a few seconds later, I felt a flood of wetness rush down the inside of her thighs as her body finally gave me what I wanted.

I grasped tight to her hips, not letting her go, pulling her on to me so that I could mercilessly trace my tongue around her clit and feel it pulsing against my lips. She was moaning softly, wriggling with the intensity of it, and, eventually, she had to reach down to push my mouth away from her pussy so that she could get a moment of relief.

"You need to learn when to hold back." She panted to me, as she pulled me to my feet and kissed me again.

"Then you shouldn't make pushing you to the edge so fun," I warned her. She giggled as she reached down to push down my underwear.

"That's not fair." She whined playfully, as I took my cock into my hand and spread her legs as wide as I could. I knew that she wanted me inside of her. There hadn't been a day that had passed since we had arrived in this place when we hadn't made love, and I knew that I was starting to get addicted to the intensity of being with her in this way. It was just ... it was just so hot to me, having her every way that I wanted her, knowing that nothing could pull us apart again.

I had been fearful that without the danger hanging over our heads, things might lose some of their spark, but if anything, all this time that we had spent together had only assured me down to the bone that this had been the right thing to do. That she was the right woman for me, and that I was the man for her. And, when we were connecting on the most carnal level that we could, there was no doubt in my mind that this was how it was meant to be. That we were always meant to find each other in this way, and that nothing was going to undo the sureness of how I felt about her.

She hooked her ankles around my back and planted her hands against my chest, looking up at me with that glimmering eagerness in her eyes. Her hair was still wet from the water, and she looked like a nymph freshly washed up from the sea.

She groaned as I pushed myself inside of her, tipping her head back and letting herself swing halfway off the rail that separated us from the ocean below. I wound my arms around her to hold her tight, and I began to move inside of her, watching as the bliss passed over her face, watching as the lust coursed through her system. I knew that she was never going to get tired of having me like this, that the two of us had bodies built to come together like this. It might have taken us a while to figure that out for good, but now that we knew, we were never going to forget it again, and I was certain of that.

I pulled her up again so that I could kiss her, wrapping my arms around her tight so that I could pull her close. There was an alchemy to her skin against mine, even after all this time, even after all this space, that I was never going to get over. I was addicted to her, deeply and fully, but it was the best addiction I'd ever had in my life. The one that made me feel alive in all the ways that mattered.

I tipped her head to face mine and kissed her again, this time, our tongues meeting slowly as I softened my pace inside of her and matched the movement of the waves behind us. She ran her hands over my scalp, catching my hair in her hands and holding tight. It had grown out the last month or so, but she told me that she liked it. And as long as she liked it, then I didn't see any point in changing it up. I was here to please her, every way that I could, and I was never going to forget that.

My hands on her waist, I fucked her in long, slow strokes, and wondered how many times we were going to have each other in this way. How many times would we still need each other so deeply? But I knew, deep down, that we would never get tired of this. We felt too good together to ever grow weary of the way our bodies felt. Mine might have been marked with scars now, with reminders of everything that we had been through, but she still loved it just the same, and I couldn't have asked for anything more than that.

She pressed her head against my chest and I could hear her breath coming faster than before. I knew that she was getting close. She was pushing back against me, her hands grabbing for whatever part of me that they could, and knowing that she was so close to the edge was everything that I needed to feel myself inching there too.

"Oh." She groaned, and I felt her pussy clench around me once more. She cried out then, a sound that seemed to get whipped away by the rush of the sea around us, and I wound my arms around her tight and lifted her off the railing so that I could push her down on top of me as far as she could go. A moment later, that rush of pleasure hit me like a ton of bricks.

"Mmm." I moaned against her ear. She had told me a few times now that she liked hearing me when we were together like this, though it had taken me a while to actually believe she meant it. She gasped, and her body tensed and froze for an instant as she clung on to me, and then she sagged into my arms. My legs were shaking for my orgasm, and I just managed to carry her back to the bed before they gave out entirely.

"Fuck." She groaned as she stretched her arms over her head and closed her eyes. "That was..."

"It was," I agreed. I knew what she was going to say. It felt as though the two of us had been working on the same wavelength since we had made it out here, and I hoped that it wasn't going to change anytime soon. I loved that we seemed to work in the same mind now. That everything that I knew I had felt about her all this time had been right.

"What do you want to do today?" I asked her, rolling over to face her, and she shook her head.

"I'm sorry, you can't make me come like that and then just act like I'm going to snap back into real-person mode," she replied, laughing. "I think I need to go back to bed for a while."

"I'm not complaining," I agreed, reaching over to pull her against my chest. In truth, I felt as though I was resting for the first time in years coming out here. I hadn't realized how much energy I had burned being constantly on guard, constantly aware that something terrible might be on the brink of happening.

But with her, right now, I could finally relax, and I intended to make the very most of it that I could. I was pretty certain that she was in no rush to get back, and I had loved every second of the time that we had passed out here. I didn't want to go back to reality. I wanted this to be our new reality, no matter what.

"I never want to leave this place," she remarked to me, propping her head up on one hand and idly tracing a finger over my chest.

"We don't have to, if you don't want to," I pointed out. "I'm pretty sure your father would keep paying for this place as long as you told him it was making up for what he did before."

"Hmm, not quite sure I have that in me." She laughed. "But it's tempting. Maybe we could do some more of the world too. That could be fun, right?"

"As long as you're there, I'm in," I replied, and I meant it. After everything that we had been through, there was only one thing that had remained true from the start, and that was that I would have done anything to keep her safe. That I would have given anything to make sure that she got everything that she wanted in life. Before, I had thought that it was just because I was being paid to take care of her, but now I could see that these feelings I'd had for her, they had been growing even back then. I had wanted to protect her because I saw something in her that went deeper than anything the rest of her family had. A pureness. A fierceness. A sureness that she was going to live her life any way that she wanted to.

And now, here she was, doing just that. And I was lucky enough that she had chosen me to share it all with her. I didn't know where the hell we went after this, but I knew that as long as she was there to keep me company, I would find a way to make it perfect.

"That's the right answer," she murmured back teasingly, planting a kiss against my chest and reaching up to run her fingers through my hair.

I gazed at her for a moment. She was beginning to dry off from her dip in the sea, her hair still a little matted from the salt. I wondered if I would ever stop being stunned by her beauty, or if it would just keep twisting me every time I laid eyes on it.

"I love you," I murmured to her, and her eyes lit up as they met mine. They always did, when I said that to her, no matter how many times she heard those words out of my lips. They never got old, it seemed.

"I love you too," she replied, and I wrapped my arms around her and pulled her close to me again. If she thought that we were done, then she had another thing coming. My mouth found hers once more, and I rolled on top of her. She smiled into the kiss, and I knew that, like me, she was probably up for a day spent cuddling and fucking in bed until the sun went down outside. Maybe a dip in the ocean to clean ourselves up once we had found our feet again, maybe order in some food to keep ourselves going and make sure that we had the energy to keep each other up all night long too.

And to me, that sounded like paradise. In fact, anything with this girl sounded like paradise to me. But here, in this secluded villa, with the sound of the waves lapping up the beach beyond us and nothing but the heat of the sun and the warmth of our bodies to distract us,

I couldn't think of anything better in the world. We might have been through hell to get here, but now, I was in heaven. And it had been worth every single step along the way to get here. That much, I was certain of. That much, I knew that I would never doubt.

THE END

Darkest Night Series

Savage
Vicious
Brutal
Sinful
Fierce

Find Lexy Timms:

LEXY TIMMS NEWSLETTER:
http://eepurl.com/9i0vD
Lexy Timms Facebook Page:
https://www.facebook.com/SavingForever
Lexy Timms Website:
http://www.lexytimms.com

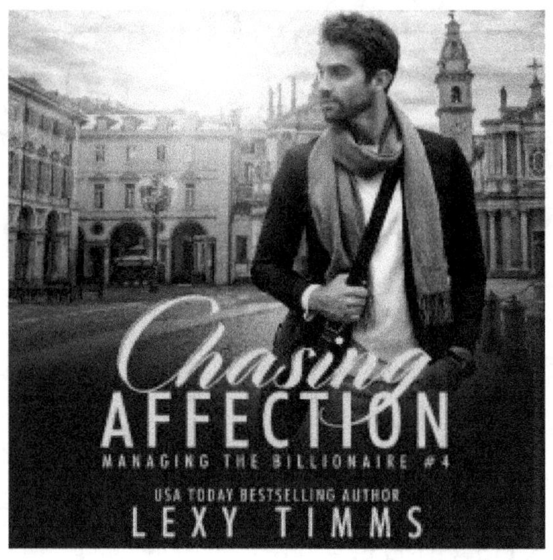
Chasing
AFFECTION
MANAGING THE BILLIONAIRE #4
USA TODAY BESTSELLING AUTHOR
LEXY TIMMS

Lexy
Timms
Managing
BOSSES
BOSS
BOSS
BOSS
FREE
for a
Limited
Time

Want

FREE READS?

Sign up for Lexy Timms' newsletter
And she'll send you updates on new releases,
ARC copies of books and a whole lotta fun!

Sign up for news and updates!
http://eepurl.com/9i0vD

More by Lexy Timms:

FROM BEST SELLING AUTHOR, Lexy Timms, comes a billionaire romance that'll make you swoon and fall in love all over again.

Jamie Connors has given up on men. Despite being smart, pretty, and just slightly overweight, she's a magnet for the kind of guys that don't stay around.

Her sister's wedding is at the foreground of the family's attention. Jamie would be fine with it if her sister wasn't pressuring her to lose weight so she'll fit in the maid of honor dress, her mother would get off her case and her ex-boyfriend wasn't about to become her brother-in-law.

Determined to step out on her own, she accepts a PA position from billionaire Alex Reid. The job includes an apartment on his property and gets her out of living in her parent's basement.

Jamie must balance her life and somehow figure out how to manage her billionaire boss, without falling in love with him.

** The Boss is book 1 in the Managing the Bosses series. All your questions won't be answered in the first book. It may end on a cliff hanger.

For mature audiences only. There are adult situations, but this is a love story, NOT erotica.

Managing the Billionaire Series

Never Enough
Worth the Cost
Secret Admirers
Chasing Affection
Pressing Romance
Timeless Memories

Faking It Description:

HE GROANED. THIS WAS torture. Being trapped in a room with a beautiful woman was just about every man's fantasy, but he had to remember that this was just pretend.

Allyson Smith has crushed on her boss for years, but never dared to make a move. When she finds herself without a date to her brother's upcoming wedding, Allyson tells her family one innocent white lie: that she's been dating her boss. Unfortunately, her boss discovers her lie, and insists on posing as her boyfriend to escort her to the wedding.

Playboy billionaire Dane Prescott always has a new heiress on his arm, but he can't get his assistant Allyson out of his head. He's fought his attraction to her, until he gets caught up in her scheme of a fake relationship.

One passionate weekend with the boss has Allyson Smith questioning everything she believes in. Falling for a wealthy playboy like Dane is against the rules, but if she's just faking it what's the harm?

THE ONE YOU CAN'T FORGET

Emily Rose Dougherty is a good Catholic girl from mythical Walkerville, CT. She had somehow managed to get herself into a heap trouble with the law, all because an ex-boyfriend has decided to make things difficult.

Luke "Spade" Wade owns a Motorcycle repair shop and is the Road Captain for Hades' Spawn MC. He's shocked when he reads in the paper that his old high school flame has been arrested. She's always been the one he couldn't forget.

Will destiny let them find each other again? Or what happens in the past, best left for the history books?

*** This is book 1 of the Hades' Spawn MC Series. All your questions may not be answered in the first book.*

Everyone
LOVES A BAD BOY
6 BOOKS BOX SET
Savage
ONE YOU CAN'T
Payment
FOR SIN
FACADE
Without
LOVE
Tattooist
LEXY TIMMS BRING YOU BOOK ONE IN SOME OF HER
BESTSELLING BAD BOY SERIES..
USA TODAY BESTSELLING AUTHOR
LEXY TIMMS

Don't miss out!

Visit the website below and you can sign up to receive emails whenever Lexy Timms publishes a new book. There's no charge and no obligation.

https://books2read.com/r/B-A-NNL-WVDHB

BOOKS 2 READ

Connecting independent readers to independent writers.

Did you love *Fierce*? Then you should read *Just About Box Set Books #1-3*[1] by Lexy Timms!

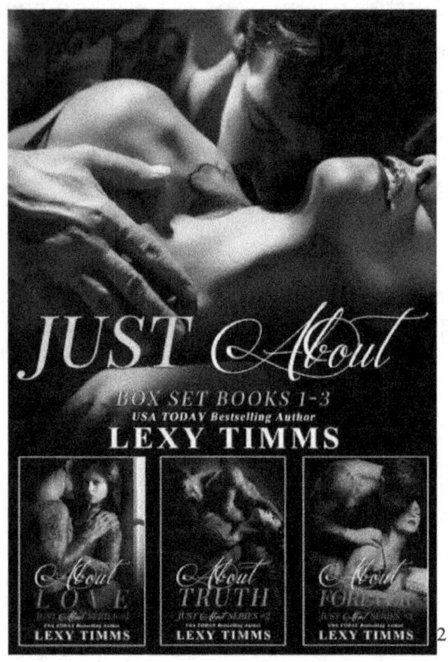

USA Today Bestselling Author, Lexy Timms, brings you a new series About Love and everything in between the road to forever.

The course of true love never did run smooth... William Shakespeare

Book 1 - About Love

After losing her money and fiancé in one go, Kellie Margolis, the one-time owner of a lucrative business, checks out of society. She needs to become something—or someone—unassuming. She's hired on as a waitress at a bar called Darkness. It's in a dangerous part of town, locally known for its Russian-American population.

---

1. https://books2read.com/u/4AKDzJ

2. https://books2read.com/u/4AKDzJ

Unexpectedly, her new life involves the erotic, shady, and incredibly charming Sasha Petrov. Sasha's too good-looking for words. Life for Kellie becomes passionate, adventurous, erotic, and bold—but by no means simple.

Though too many signals say Sasha plays dirty, Kellie decides she'd be a fool to deny herself the pleasure he brings her. Their affair becomes more like a fairy tale, and Kellie starts believing Sasha is the love she deserves after her hard times. When Kellie's past unexpectedly comes full circle, she realizes how small the world really is.

Will an unforeseen discovery break Kellie's heart for good, or will Sasha be the bad boy hero he's set himself up to be?

<u>Book 2 - About Truth</u>

What could be sexier than a smoking-hot Russian man built like a brick house? One who is so into you...

High on a hot, romantic love affair, young and pretty Kallie Margolis has everything—almost. She has a beautiful house, all the money she needs, and the undivided attention of the most magnificent man she could ever imagine. Only, she doesn't have to just imagine him because Sasha Petrov is gorgeous, larger than life, unbelievable in bed, and very real.

Sasha is also the one who unwittingly helped ruin everything Kallie once had, and still she fell for him. He earns his living on the mean streets of Baltimore in ways Kallie doesn't want to know. Their animal need for one another rockets them way beyond all that, and they have the time of their lives as Sasha makes it all up to her.

Just when the world could not get rosier, their passion more off the hook, the bottom threatens to drop out. Has Sasha played Kallie for a fool? Is he going to take her for another ride? Or can Kallie trust the sensual bad boy when he says his for love her, not a life of crime, is what drives him?

<u>Book 3 - About Forever</u>

There comes a time, even in the hottest relationship ever, when enough is enough. But cutting off the magnificent and gorgeous bad boy Sasha Petrov is like cutting off an arm; Kallie Margolis just can't do it. His dangerous charm and once-in-a-lifetime passion. If anyone had told her before she left town on the fly that Sasha wasn't right for her, she couldn't even imagine it.

But once again, Kallie finds herself waking up in rustic, beach-front digs trying to make sense of it all. Getting away to sort it out isn't an option, because Sasha is always one step behind. He lures her back into his powerful arms just by being near. He tries being cold and callous to teach her a lesson for taking off, but he can no more be angry with her than she can break up with him. When things look like they're going to straighten out for the two of them the never-been-caught street-smart Sasha is arrested, this time for a fairly serious crime.

He's a self-employed businessman who unapologetically deals with things not quite legal. Will the fallout of his shady pursuits be the end of the sweetest love Kallie believes she will ever find? Or will Sasha beat the odds and make it back to Kallie's bed, and into her heart for good?

Read more at www.lexytimms.com.

Also by Lexy Timms

A Bad Boy Bullied Romance
I Hate You
I Hate You A Little Bit
I Hate You A Little Bit More

A Burning Love Series
Spark of Passion
Flame of Desire
Blaze of Ecstasy

A Chance at Forever Series
Forever Perfect
Forever Desired
Forever Together

A Dating App Series
I've Been Matched
You've Been Matched

We've Been Matched

A "Kind of" Billionaire
Taking a Risk
Safety in Numbers
Pretend You're Mine

A Maybe Series
Maybe I Should
Maybe I Shouldn't
Maybe I Did

Assisting the Boss Series
Billion Reasons
Duke of Delegation
Late Night Meetings
Delegating Love
Suitors and Admirers

BBW Romance Series
Capturing Her Beauty
Pursuing Her Dreams
Tracing Her Curves

Beating the Biker Series
Making Her His
Making the Break
Making of Them

Billionaire Banker Series
Banking on Him
Price of Passion
Investing in Love
Knowing Your Worth
Treasured Forever
Banking on Christmas

Billionaire Holiday Romance Series
Driving Home for Christmas
The Valentine Getaway
Cruising Love

Billionaire in Disguise Series
Facade
Illusion
Charade

Billionaire Secrets Series

The Secret
Freedom
Courage
Trust
Impulse
Billionaire Secrets Box Set Books #1-3

Blind Sight Series
See Me
Fix Me
Eyes On Me

Branded Series
Money or Nothing
What People Say
Give and Take

Building Billions
Building Billions - Part 1
Building Billions - Part 2
Building Billions - Part 3

Butler & Heiress Series
To Serve
For Duty
No Chore

Change of Heart Series
The Heart Needs
The Heart Wants
The Heart Knows

Conquering Warrior Series
Ruthless

Counting the Billions
Counting the Days
Counting On You
Counting the Kisses

Darkest Night Series
Savage
Vicious
Brutal
Sinful
Fierce

Diamond in the Rough Anthology
Billionaire Rock
Billionaire Rock - part 2

Dirty Little Taboo Series
Flirting Touch
Denying Pleasure
Forbidding Desire
Craving Passion

Dominating PA Series
Her Personal Assistant - Part 1
Her Personal Assistant Box Set

Fake Billionaire Series
Faking It
Temporary CEO
Caught in the Act
Never Tell A Lie
Fake Christmas
Fake Billionaire Box Set #1-3

Firehouse Romance Series
Caught in Flames
Burning With Desire
Craving the Heat
Firehouse Romance Complete Collection

Forging Billions Series
Dirty Money
Petty Cash
Payment Required

For His Pleasure
Elizabeth
Georgia
Madison

Fortune Riders MC Series
Billionaire Biker
Billionaire Ransom
Billionaire Misery
Fortune Riders Box Set - Books #1-3

Fragile Series
Fragile Touch
Fragile Kiss
Fragile Love

Great Temptation Series
The Devil's Footsteps
Heaven's Command

Mortals Surrender

Hades' Spawn Motorcycle Club
One You Can't Forget
One That Got Away
One That Came Back
One You Never Leave
One Christmas Night
Hades' Spawn MC Complete Series

Hard Rocked Series
Rhyme
Harmony
Lyrics

Heart of Stone Series
The Protector
The Guardian
The Warrior

Heart of the Battle Series
Celtic Viking
Celtic Rune
Celtic Mann
Heart of the Battle Series Box Set

Heistdom Series
Master Thief
Goldmine
Diamond Heist
Smile For Me
Your Move
Green With Envy
Saving Money

Highlander Wolf Series
Pack Run
Pack Land
Pack Rules

How To Love A Spy
The Secret
The Secret Life
The Secret Wife

Just About Series
About Love
About Truth
About Forever
Just About Box Set Books #1-3

Justice Series
Seeking Justice
Finding Justice
Chasing Justice
Pursuing Justice
Justice - Complete Series

Kissed by Billions
Kissed by Passion
Kissed by Desire
Kissed by Love

Leaning Towards Trouble
Trouble
Discord
Tenacity

Love on the Sea Series
Ships Ahoy
Rough Sea
High Tide

Love You Series
Love Life

Need Love
My Love

Managing the Billionaire
Never Enough
Worth the Cost
Secret Admirers
Chasing Affection
Pressing Romance
Timeless Memories
Managing the Billionaire Box Set Books #1-3

Managing the Bosses Series
The Boss
The Boss Too
Who's the Boss Now
Love the Boss
I Do the Boss
Wife to the Boss
Employed by the Boss
Brother to the Boss
Senior Advisor to the Boss
Forever the Boss
Christmas With the Boss
Billionaire in Control
Billionaire Makes Millions
Billionaire at Work
Precious Little Thing
Priceless Love
Valentine Love

The Cost of Freedom
Trick or Treat
The Night Before Christmas
Gift for the Boss - Novella 3.5
Managing the Bosses Box Set #1-3
Managing the Bosses Novellas

Mislead by the Bad Boy Series
Deceived
Provoked
Betrayed

Model Mayhem Series
Shameless
Modesty
Imperfection

Moment in Time
Highlander's Bride
Victorian Bride
Modern Day Bride
A Royal Bride
Forever the Bride

My Best Friend's Sister
Hometown Calling

A Perfect Moment
Thrown in Together

My Darker Side Series
Darkest Hour
Time to Stop
Against the Light

Neverending Dream Series
Neverending Dream - Part 1
Neverending Dream - Part 2
Neverending Dream - Part 3
Neverending Dream - Part 4
Neverending Dream - Part 5

Outside the Octagon
Submit
Fight
Knockout

Protecting Diana Series
Her Bodyguard
Her Defender
Her Champion
Her Protector
Her Forever

Protecting Layla Series
His Mission
His Objective
His Devotion

Racing Hearts Series
Rush
Pace
Fast

Regency Romance Series
The Duchess Scandal - Part 1
The Duchess Scandal - Part 2

Reverse Harem Series
Primals
Archaic
Unitary

RIP Series
Track the Ripper
Hunt the Ripper
Pursue the Ripper

R&S Rich and Single Series
Alex Reid
Parker

Saving Forever
Saving Forever - Part 1
Saving Forever - Part 2
Saving Forever - Part 3
Saving Forever - Part 4
Saving Forever - Part 5
Saving Forever - Part 6
Saving Forever Part 7
Saving Forever - Part 8
Saving Forever Boxset Books #1-3

Shifting Desires Series
Jungle Heat
Jungle Fever
Jungle Blaze

Sin Series
Payment for Sin
Atonement Within
Declaration of Love

Southern Romance Series
Little Love Affair
Siege of the Heart
Freedom Forever
Soldier's Fortune

Spanked Series
Passion
Playmate
Pleasure

Spelling Love Series
The Author
The Book Boyfriend
The Words of Love

Taboo Wedding Series
He Loves Me Not
With This Ring
Happily Ever After

Tattooist Series
Confession of a Tattooist
Surrender of a Tattooist

Heart of a Tattooist
Hopes & Dreams of a Tattooist

Tennessee Romance
Whisky Lullaby
Whisky Melody
Whisky Harmony

The Bad Boy Alpha Club
Battle Lines - Part 1
Battle Lines

The Brush Of Love Series
Every Night
Every Day
Every Time
Every Way
Every Touch
The Brush of Love Series Box Set Books #1-3

The Debt
The Debt: Part 1 - Damn Horse
The Debt: Complete Collection

The Sound of Breaking Hearts Series
Disruption
Destroy
Devoted

The University of Gatica Series
The Recruiting Trip
Faster
Higher
Stronger
Dominate
No Rush
University of Gatica - The Complete Series

T.N.T. Series
Troubled Nate Thomas - Part 1
Troubled Nate Thomas - Part 2
Troubled Nate Thomas - Part 3

Toxic Touch Series
Noxious
Lethal
Willful
Tainted
Craved

Undercover Series
Perfect For Me
Perfect For You
Perfect For Us

Unknown Identity Series
Unknown
Unpublished
Unexposed
Unsure
Unwritten
Unknown Identity Box Set: Books #1-3

Unlucky Series
Unlucky in Love
UnWanted
UnLoved Forever

War Torn Letters Series
My Sweetheart
My Darling
My Beloved

Wet & Wild Series

Stormy Love
Savage Love
Secure Love

Worth It Series
Worth Billions
Worth Every Cent
Worth More Than Money

You & Me - A Bad Boy Romance
Just Me
Touch Me
Kiss Me

Standalone
Wash
Loving Charity
Summer Lovin'
Love & College
Billionaire Heart
First Love
Frisky and Fun Romance Box Collection
Beating Hades' Bikers

About the Author

"Love should be something that lasts forever, not is lost forever." Visit USA TODAY BESTSELLING AUTHOR, LEXY TIMMS https://www.facebook.com/SavingForever *Please feel free to connect with me and share your comments. I love connecting with my readers.* Sign up for news and updates and freebies - I like spoiling my readers! http://eepurl.com/9i0vD website: www.lexytimms.com Dealing in Antique Jewelry and hanging out with her awesome hubby and three kids, Lexy Timms loves writing in her free time. MANAGING THE BOSSES is a bestselling 10-part series dipping into the lives of Alex Reid and Jamie Connors. Can a secretary really fall for her billionaire boss?

Read more at www.lexytimms.com.